NOBODY'S DARLING

A Nobody Romance

Other books by Gina Ardito:

The Money Romance Series
The Bonds of Matri-Money
A Run for the Money

NOBODY'S DARLING

•

Gina Ardito

AVALON BOOKS
NEW YORK

Published by Avalon Books,
an imprint of Thomas Bouregy & Co., Inc.
160 Madison Avenue, New York, NY 10016

Library of Congress Cataloging-in-Publication Data

Ardito, Gina.
  Nobody's darling / Gina Ardito.
       p. cm.
    ISBN 978-0-8034-7722-3
  1. Businesswomen—Fiction.   2. Television personalities—
Fiction.   3. Reality television programs—Fiction.   I. Title.
    PS3601.R43N63 2011
    813'.6—dc22

                                             2010037152

PRINTED IN THE UNITED STATES OF AMERICA
ON ACID-FREE PAPER
BY RR DONNELLEY, BLOOMSBURG, PENNSYLVANIA

*For Gail Rodgers, who's not only the ultimate Superwoman,
she's the greatest friend. I love ya, my Southern belle!*

Chapter One

"Everyone is looking for a mother to care for them."

The moment the sentence left her lips, April Raine wanted to take it back. Instead, though, she squirmed on the couch in the faux living room set of daytime talk show *Taking Sides*. She chalked up the unexpected slip to nerves stretched tighter than her panty hose.

One size fits all, my butt. One size fits all anorexic runway models, maybe.

While her waistband dug trenches into her old C-section scar, the klieg lights burned down, beading sweat on her upper lip. She could almost hear crickets chirping in the canyon of silence around her.

"Wow, April." Grant Harrison, on her right, sat up higher in his armchair. "You don't really mean that, do you?"

Backpedaling would only make her look desperate. Seeing no other choice, she opted to keep the conversation light and hope the audience took her comment in stride. "I guess I do, Grant. I've built an entire business around that theory."

"Let's talk about that," Jocelyn Jones, the cohost seated directly across from her, interjected. "Several years ago, you were a married woman with what you thought was the perfect life. Then one day your husband ran off with another woman, leaving you destitute and facing eviction."

Wham! Did somebody catch the license plate number of that truck? Taking Sides had a reputation for kamikaze interviews, but Jocelyn's statement hit way below the belt. Actually, it was more like a blow to the shoulder blades with a two-by-four.

1

Well, if total strangers were about to learn the details of her private pain, they'd hear the unvarnished truth and not some detached two-sentence summary.

"My financial downturn didn't exactly occur within forty-eight hours of my husband's departure. I struggled for years to make ends meet, worked at dozens of low-paying jobs, pawned everything of value I owned. I did whatever I could to keep my family solvent. . . ."

"That must have been very difficult for you." Jocelyn patted her hand sympathetically. The gesture played well for the cameras but left April stone cold, and she pulled away to avoid further contact.

Never missing a beat, Jocelyn transformed her sharklike mien to puppy eagerness. "Until you started your own business. How exactly did you come up with the idea for Rainey-Day-Wife?"

Good. Let's get this interview on the topic of business, rather than my personal life.

"A neighbor of mine had to work overtime on a night he was responsible for carpooling his son's soccer team. He asked if I would drive the team. In exchange, he offered to pay my expenses plus a little extra for doing the favor on a moment's notice."

Grant flashed his trademark smile at the audience. "And, ladies and gentlemen, from that simple errand six years ago, April Raine built a thriving company. Isn't that incredible?"

Boisterous applause rose from the studio audience.

April sidled to the edge of her seat to be heard over the noise. "Once again, it didn't happen overnight," she said. "I had to—"

"Now," Grant interrupted, "you have dozens of clients who hire you on a month-to-month basis to handle their families' needs, isn't that correct?"

"Well . . . yes."

"And what sort of tasks does Rainey-Day-Wife perform?"

April shrugged. "Anything your average wife does."

"Anything?" Waggling his brows, he leaned close.

She pinned her hands beneath her thighs to keep from smacking the leer off his face. A line from an old movie popped into her head. It came from her idol, Bette Davis, in *Beyond the Forest*:

"Life in Loyalton is like sitting in the funeral parlor and waiting for the funeral to begin. No, it's like lying in a coffin and waiting for them to carry you out."

Well, as long as April had some life in her legs, no one would carry her out without a struggle.

Assuming her best Bette Davis poise, she replied, "What I mean is we handle the day-to-day errands that pile up. Carpooling, grocery shopping, housework, driving to extracurricular activities, picking up dry cleaning and even prescriptions. We bake cupcakes, help with homework, and stay with sick children. A true wife wears a multitude of hats every day. Chauffeur, chef, tutor, maid, nurse. It's all in a day's work. Since our customers expect a variety of services, Rainey-Day-Wife consists of individuals trained in all aspects of family life."

"Could you give us an example?" Jocelyn asked.

Tilting her head, April considered her mental list of stressed-out parents. "Well, we have one client who, twice a month, requires someone to make Sunday dinner."

"Wouldn't it be easier to eat out?" Grant asked.

She shrugged. "Maybe. But this father misses the family dinners of his youth and wants his children to grow up with that tradition. If our staff member handles the dirty work, he gets the chance to reconnect with his little ones without the stress of preparing a big meal." She leaned forward, her hands folded in her lap. "You must understand: this gentleman only sees his children two weekends per month, alternate holidays, and one month during summer vacation. He's a member of what I call the fast-food group. Some of these dads consider zapping a TV dinner in the microwave home cooking."

The audience tittered. Through the almost blinding lights, April noticed a few women nodding in agreement.

"But you don't deal strictly with single dads, do you?" Jocelyn asked.

"No, although I'd say about seventy percent of our clients fit that profile. We have a few single moms and several busy couples. But my experience is that most women juggle the responsibilities of parenting better than men." Was that too sexist? Maybe. But in her experience, it was true. Still, she might want to take a moment for quick damage control. "Regardless of gender, however, all families run into crunch times where there just aren't enough hours in the day. Whether our clients opt for a long-term contract or temporary help, Rainey-Day-Wife is there to make their burdens a little easier."

"Yet there are those who disapprove of your business," Jocelyn said. "Most notably, our very own Dr. Jefferson Prentiss, who placed your company at the top of his annual list of the Most Family-Unfriendly Businesses in New York two years in a row. Isn't that right?"

"Three, actually," April said, correcting her with a grim smile.

Every December, Dr. Jeff put her on his cockamamie list, and she lost 30 percent of her business come January. Oh, she always recouped by the second quarter, but she couldn't afford to continue going through this year after year. That explained why she'd agreed to go along with this current madness.

"And we're in for a very spirited debate on the matter, as Dr. Jeff is here with us today," Jocelyn announced, rising to her feet. "Ladies and gentlemen, please welcome *New York Times* bestselling author and frequent *Taking Sides* guest Dr. Jefferson Prentiss."

He strolled onstage to the appreciative cheers of every woman in the audience. It was no wonder.

The photo on his book jacket didn't do him justice. Glossy black curls framed a face fit for a rock star. His shoulders, encased in a pale blue shadow-striped shirt, looked broader than her backyard clothesline. He shook hands with the hosts, then turned his attention to her.

Smoky gray eyes behind thick sooty lashes drew her in with hypnotic power as he bent to shake her hand. His warm clasp reflected his posture, which indicated that he was completely at ease with the gushing adoration of the females inside the studio. Then he gave her a slow wink, and her jaw dropped to chest level.

"Pleased to meet you," he murmured in a voice richer than hot chocolate on a wintry afternoon.

"Same here," she managed to reply through a throat cloaked in a blanket of nerves.

He took a seat beside her, so close his thigh pressed against hers, and she scooched up near the arm of the couch. The skin tightened around her bones, leaving her fearful that if she inhaled too deeply, her skeleton might snap in two.

The moment the applause and catcalls died down, Jocelyn said, "Dr. Jeff, you believe that businesses like Rainey-Day-Wife contribute to the breakdown of families."

Dr. Jeff shook his head at April, then faced the audience. "Yes, I'm afraid so, Jocelyn. Such an enterprise not only takes advantage of the greatest tragedy of family life, the specter of divorce, but it also gives parents a way to avoid their obligations to their children. Ms. Raine may call it whatever she likes—a business, a service—but her company and others like it profit from their clients' heartache. They have no conscience, never giving a second thought to how their mercenary practices contribute to a child's loss of structure and security. I find that shameful."

Wait a minute. Had he just called her mercenary? Nervousness and thoughts of making a good impression disappeared. In their place a good, healthy umbrage simmered in April's veins. She opened her mouth to retort, but Jocelyn beat her to it.

"Still, Ms. Raine had no education and no career skills. Alternatives must have been very difficult to come by. Don't you think she had an obligation to provide for her children in any way she could?"

"At the expense of other families' happiness?" Dr. Jeff rejoined. "Surely a woman as enterprising as Ms. Raine could find a way to make a living that did not require her to alienate parents from their children and wives from their husbands." He leaned over the knifelike creases in his gray slacks, hands outstretched toward the camera. "This is exactly what's wrong with today's world. Our society has broken down to the point where the simple acts of love and consideration that should be part of everyday life are handled by profit-seeking strangers, rather than family members. I'm appalled that an intelligent woman like today's guest feels no shame collecting a salary while destroying relationships."

April squirmed some more, fisting her hands until her fingernails dug painfully into her palms. Oh, she'd love to blast him with all the fire simmering in her belly's furnace. But that would only set off the audience, and this interview was supposed to bring positive publicity to Rainey-Day-Wife.

"Take, for instance, Ms. Raine's client who requires the Sunday dinner," Dr. Jeff continued. "Would it be so terrible if that dad cooked the meal himself? Perhaps he might even allow his children to participate in small ways. A four-year-old can help set a table. Older children might prepare a salad or dry the dishes after the meal. These are the special moments that bring families together."

"You raise some interesting points, as always," Grant said, then turned to April. "Do you wish to reply to Dr. Jeff's comments?"

You bet I do!

Tamping down visions of slow roasting a naked, trussed-up Dr. Jeff on a rotisserie, she edged forward on the couch. "Yes, Grant, thank you."

Before April might take advantage of her opportunity, Jocelyn held up a hand. "Well, we'll give you a chance to do so right after this commercial break."

The *Taking Sides* theme music swelled around the stage, and from somewhere beyond the blinding white lights, a deep voice announced, "And we're out. Two minutes, people."

Chapter Two

As the studio broke for commercial, Jeff Prentiss turned his gaze to Ms. Raine. She scrunched against the end of the couch as if he were a serial killer holding a dripping knife.

He flashed a reassuring smile. "You're doing great."

"Thanks," she mumbled, but her eyes narrowed in his direction, declaring him the enemy.

By God, how he regretted the day he'd signed the contract to be a regular guest here. At the lowest point in his life, when his judgment was off-kilter, too many vultures circled his carcass, ready to take advantage of his weakness.

His partners reveled in the publicity of being associated with "Dr. Jeff from *Taking Sides*." They saw their patient load increase by at least 50 percent a year. The show's producers rejoiced at their higher ratings. And after each of his appearances, his book sales increased dramatically, making his editor delirious.

Meanwhile, every time Jeff left the soundstage, his mind calculated how many more episodes he'd have to endure before the end of his contract. After all, he wasn't in this for the money or the fame. Money and fame couldn't banish heartbreak, depression, or any of the other demons his patients faced. Quite simply, this television show was the best vehicle for reaching as many potential victims of the demons as possible.

Yet he always had the impression that the show's producers didn't care about his credentials. They simply considered him the pretty boy of psychology.

On the subject of pretty . . . April Raine was a pleasant surprise. Based on her business profile, he'd expected a plump, matronly woman—the grandma type, who wore floral housecoats and baked more cookies than the Keebler elves. A pushover, as Rodney, his agent, had tagged her.

The curvaceous woman in the burgundy suit and white blouse contrasted sharply with his imagination's picture. Served him right for jumping to conclusions, he supposed.

That was another reason to look forward to his last appearance on this stage. He was spending too much time with Jocelyn and Grant, getting jaded. . . .

Of course, he should have revised his opinion after reading April Raine's bio for today's show. She didn't have the history of a pushover. Anyone who could pull herself out of poverty and become a successful businesswoman—with only a GED to her educational credit—had more guts than an army battalion.

He took a moment to study the face above her collar. It was pert, pretty, younger than he'd expected. According to what he'd read about her, she had an eighteen-year-old daughter. Yet she barely looked old enough to be out of high school herself. Her chestnut hair was cut in a fun style that flipped up at her determined little chin. Cinnamon freckles peeked through the studio's makeup on her nose and cheeks.

Honey-colored eyes filled with distrust, however, communicated anger at his opening remarks. No problem. He knew how to put perturbed people at ease.

"Really, I'm impressed," he said. "These two thrive on making guests look like morons, but you're not falling for it. Good for you."

Instead of becoming more relaxed at his compliment, she backed up farther away from him. Odd, since he hadn't realized that was possible on the cramped sofa they shared. Worse, she fixed him with a stare so cold that polar bears could swim in her eyes.

"What game are you playing, Doctor? Do you think if you're nice to me now, I'll be nice to *you* when the cameras are turned on again?"

"There's no need to feel defensive with me," he said reassuringly. "The producers want a lively debate, since we approach today's topic from drastically different angles. My comments aren't meant to insult you. Just relax and have fun, okay?"

She gave him a tight-lipped smile in reply. Before he could say anything else, the lights flashed, and the intro music sang.

"We're back." Jocelyn spoke to the camera. "In case you've just joined us, we're talking with Ms. April Raine, founder of Rainey-Day-Wife, a parenting services organization, and Dr. Jefferson Prentiss, author of *Love Is a Contact Sport*. Now, April, you said you wanted to respond to Dr. Jeff's comments about your organization's negative impact on marriage and family."

"Yes, Jocelyn, thank you." She turned a steady gaze toward him. "First of all, I'd like to say there's nothing mercenary or shameful in what I do. I provide a service to families who need help, and I am compensated for that service. Don't you profit from the problems of others, including problems due to troubled relationships?"

Jeff frowned. "I hardly see that as the same thing."

"No? Do you only treat healthy, well-adjusted patients?"

"Of course not." Where was she headed with this? "But my practice is geared toward healing their ills, not taking advantage of them."

"And if you can't heal those ills, do you waive your fees? Are you a philanthropist, Dr. Prentiss?"

"I'm an educated professional, Ms. Raine."

Her only reaction to the barb was the quick blink of her eyes. But with a steady voice, she replied, "I've read your book, you know. Unfortunately, I found vital information missing."

"Oh?" He arched a brow at her. "Such as?"

"Such as a successful relationship takes two people"—she held up two fingers in front of his face—"working together, twenty-four hours a day, three hundred and sixty-five days a year. Endlessly loving rapport with a spouse is not easy to attain. Bette Davis once said, 'Love is not enough. It must be the foundation, the cornerstone—but not the complete structure. It is much too pliable, too yielding.'"

His frown deepened until he sensed the camera zooming in, and he changed his expression to casual. "If you read my book, you'd know I never claimed loving rapport was easy. Nothing worthwhile in life is easy to attain. Certainly, by the time a couple decides to have a family, however, they should be secure in their partnership and ready to face new challenges."

Shaking her head, she smiled, as if she knew a secret he wasn't privy to. "No one can fully prepare for the stresses of parenthood. Whenever a child is born, priorities change, and a couple's life is irrevocably altered. Raising a family is the most difficult, gut-wrenching job two people can attempt. Sometimes, the experience makes them stronger. Other times, it tears them apart. But whether their partnership succeeds or fails after the arrival of children, no one's life should be judged by the outcome."

Several ladies in the audience cheered, and their hoots and whoops echoed off the soundstage.

Jeff leaned back and waited for the volume in the room to return to normal before continuing. "I realize how demanding a parent's role is these days. That's why my book stresses that couples must maintain a relationship based on infinite acts of love and consideration, toward each other as well as their children. So they don't find themselves abandoned, juggling too many responsibilities, and ignoring their children's true needs in the process."

Her voice grew soft, almost sympathetic. "How much experience do you have juggling responsibilities, Doctor?"

Now he blinked. "I'm sorry?"

"Have you ever lost a job because you stayed home with a sick child once too often?" she demanded. "When was the last time you tried to balance your attention evenly between your spouse, your children, your boss, your home, and yourself? Have you ever spent a sleepless night worrying that the check you sent to the gas company would clear your account before your deposit did? Parents are often stretched so tight it's a wonder more of us don't snap. Frankly, my services help save families teetering on the edge of a breakdown, because my staff and I offer them the gift of time. And every parent, no matter how devoted to family, benefits more from extra time than from the acts of love and consideration you espouse."

Her words stung like sleet, pelting him with righteous anger.

"April," Grant interjected, his uneasy gaze swinging from one opponent to the other, "you're heading off the subject—"

Jeff held up a hand. "No, that's quite all right, Grant. I find Ms. Raine's opinions refreshing, if a trifle naïve."

"Naïve? Me? I beg to differ, Doctor. Look at your shoes, for goodness sake."

"My shoes?" He stared at his black calf-leather oxfords curiously. "What's wrong with my shoes?"

"Nothing. As a matter of fact, they're quite nice."

Her gaze moved from his feet to his face. Pity shimmered in her eyes. He bit back a grimace. Of all the emotions in the human repertoire, he despised pity most, perhaps because he'd been the subject of so much of it after Emma's death.

"For the first three years after my husband left me," she whispered, "I didn't spend a dime on myself. Most days, I wore a pair of moccasins I'd found at a garage sale. My children needed food, health care, clothing, and a roof over their heads. Those necessities took priority over my worn-out shoes. While I agree children need family stability, other needs require just as much attention. And parents, whether single or married, do the best they can to tend to all those needs. I resent your criticizing my vocation, which does nothing more than attempt to lighten the load for those who are overwhelmed. Most of all, though, I resent your assumption that if I'd kissed my husband's lily-white butt more often, I wouldn't have found myself broke and alone."

The audience erupted in wild applause, hoots, and cheers.

Despite the sizzle of her impassioned speech and the boisterous reaction of the audience, he kept his tone even, professional. "Touché, Ms. Raine, but I think you're misinterpreting my professional opinion as a personal attack—"

"And I think you want a female society of mindless robots hearkening back to the good old days when we were all barefoot, pregnant, and stuck in the kitchen."

"Now hold on." Grant intervened again with a chuckle. "We can't allow you to come to fisticuffs over this. Besides, we've devised the solution to satisfy you both."

Jocelyn leaned toward the nearest camera, her hands folded neatly on the curve of her knees. "As some of you may be aware, Harmony House was originally built to assist troubled couples in working out their marital problems in seclusion."

"Some seclusion," Ms. Raine murmured. But her mike amplified her words. "With hidden cameras and microphones in every room. A million television viewers watching your every private moment—"

"Nevertheless," Grant said, cutting her off, "the participants of the Harmony House experiments have reported tremendous success each season. Now *Taking Sides* has acquired the property for a little experiment of our own."

"Ladies and gentlemen"—Jocelyn's voice grew breathless with excitement—"both Dr. Jeff and Ms. Raine have agreed to our challenge. For the next thirty days, they'll live together at Harmony House. Each day, you, the audience, will have the ability to see highlights of their time together, to judge for yourself. Can Dr. Jeff convince you that any relationship—even a contradictory one—benefits from infinite acts of love and consideration? Or will Ms. Raine prove that no amount of love and consideration can ease the strain the modern world puts on a couple?"

"The best part," Grant concluded, "is that the winner will receive one hundred thousand dollars, furnished by our sponsors. So . . . let the battle of the sexes begin!"

Chapter Three

Inside the kitchen of Snowed Inn Bed and Breakfast, Brooklyn Raine Cheviot watched television while washing the morning's dishes. Normally she avoided the daytime talk shows, but when her older sister Summer had called to tell her about April's interview on *Taking Sides,* Lyn had noted the date on her calendar with a fat red Sharpie.

Sure enough, there was April, giving as good as she got to that pompous Dr. Jeff character. Flashing a soapy thumbs-up, Lyn silently cheered her big sister. Of the three of them, April had the most guts, the most determination.

Their parents had always seen April as a disappointment, had overlooked her successes to harp on her mistakes. And of course, Lyn's stellar achievements—and the subsequent accolades from Dad—didn't help bridge the gap between her and her sister.

Lyn would give back all her medals, would gladly forget all the accolades she'd ever received, for just one ounce of April's courage in the face of adversity.

Lyn's oldest sister had accomplished so much in her life. She lacked a high school diploma, and she'd had a bad marriage, a vicious divorce, and issues with her son, but April had somehow managed to bounce back from all those tragedies—to not only bounce back, but soar above them.

Why can't I?

She clenched her fingers into a tight fist. *Tink!* The juice glass in her hand shattered, slicing two of her fingers with the shards.

Dagnabbit.

Blood dripped onto the white stoneware soaking in the sink, creating perfect Rorschach images of her pain and loneliness. Her eyes filling with tears yet again, Lyn turned off the faucet and picked up the broken pieces of glass. If only she could as easily pick up the broken pieces of her life.

In her dorm room at the state university, Rebecca Jayne Donovan curled up on her bed and watched her mother's first television appearance. Across the scarred floorboards, her roommate straddled her desk chair.

"That's your mom?" Evie asked. Without waiting for a reply, she added, "She looks cool."

Cool? Hardly. Becky had never seen her mother so lit up. Where had that fire come from? Oh, sure, Mom always knew how to hold her own against Dad or Grandma. Even Aunt Summer and Aunt Lyn were used to bowing to Mom's argumentative nature. But the woman involved in a heated debate with Dr. Jeff was a stranger.

Mom always projected that perfect business attitude. She never let Becky forget that every person she met was a potential client.

Yet there she was, in living color on the teeny twenty-one-inch television. Becky narrowed her eyes and totally focused on the couple seated on the talk show's couch. With her body swiveled toward the psychiatrist, her hands clutched in her lap, and her normally warm eyes smoldering with some bizarre volcanic fire, Mom's whole posture seemed off. And the doctor's knees were pointed toward Mom's, his bearing a little more relaxed, and his gaze pinned on her.

A warm flush of embarrassment crept up Becky's neck, but her gaze remained fixed on the couple on the screen. They looked so focused on each other . . .

No. It couldn't be . . .

If Becky were watching any other couple, she'd swear these two were totally hot for each other. But this was her mom!

"I think she likes him," Evie said.

Becky's attention swerved from the screen to her roommate. "Oh, God," she groaned. "Is it that obvious?"

Men and women are genetically predisposed to their roles in society. Whether you believe in Creation as an act of a supreme being or in Darwin's theory of evolution, the underlying message is the same. Throughout history, man has been the provider, the hunter, the progenitor. Woman's role is the child bearer, the nurturer, the keeper of the hearth.

In recent years, humanity has tried to blur these divisions of the sexes. The result has been widespread decimation of the family unit. An increase in divorce, physical and emotional abuse, substance abuse, and self-loathing can be linked to this attempt to change our inherent natures. . . .

April slammed the book closed and resisted the urge to toss it across the room. Too bad. She would have loved to hear the satisfying thud when it collided with her bedroom wall. Instead, she punched the pillows behind her back until they resembled lumpy, floral-covered hills across the lacquered headboard.

What a quack. How could any female buy into his malarkey? According to Dr. Jefferson Prentiss, all society's ills lay squarely at the feet of the women's movement.

She'd hoped to find in the pages a clue to what made Dr. Jeff tick, something to use to her advantage when she began living with him—tomorrow.

But did she find a chink in his armor? Of course not. That would be too easy. And nothing was ever easy for April.

A sharp rap on the door brought her eyes up.

"Mom?" It was Mike's muffled voice.

"Come on in, honey," she called out.

The door opened, and in bounded one of the two lights of her life. "Okay if I sit with you for a while?"

Careful not to wrinkle her skirt, she slid over and patted the empty space beside her on the queen-size bed. "You bet."

Mike needed no additional encouragement. He scrambled up

and placed his sandy-haired head on her shoulder. With a deep sigh of contentment, April wrapped an arm around his skinny frame and squeezed.

"Mom," he whined. "You're crushing me."

Though she wanted nothing more than to hold him, to protect him from all the evils of the world, she relaxed her grip and allowed him some breathing room.

"Daddy should be here to pick you up soon. You all packed?"

"Uh-huh," he replied. "Are you?"

"Mmm-hmm," she answered, offering the same wealth of information.

His exhaled breath wafted upwards from her collarbone, warm and sweet, bubble gum scented. "I wish I were going with you. If I'm not there, who's gonna take care of you?"

She smiled at his protective tone. Since Peter had walked out, her son had regarded his position as male head of the household very seriously, despite his handicap—or maybe because of it.

"Don't worry about me. I'll be fine."

When Mike scowled, she poked him between the ribs with a pair of wiggling fingers until he burst into laughter. His slender body squirmed against her, and his knees drew up to his chest in a fetal position. "Stop, Mom," he pleaded. "Stop."

The *bing-bong* of the doorbell broke them apart.

One last smile in her direction and Michael scrambled off the bed. "I bet that's Dad."

"Oh, goody," April muttered.

While he raced downstairs to open the front door, she rose from the bed and checked her reflection in the full-length mirror. Grateful she'd squeezed in that appointment at the salon for a touch-up yesterday, she fluffed the edges of her hair with extended fingers. The sweater and skirt ensemble she wore hid a multitude of sins—not the least of which was that itty bit of abdominal flab that no amount of yoga or crunches could flatten.

The effect her looks had on Peter had reigned uppermost in her mind for almost twenty years. The shaming betrayals, the lean days she'd suffered through until the court had ordered monthly child-support payments, his boomerang marriage to Lori a mere eight weeks after the ink dried on their divorce decree—none of that mattered. Well, yes, on second thought, it did matter. The flutter she experienced now had more to do with agitation than attraction.

What had Bette Davis said? "Men become much more attractive when they start looking older. But it doesn't do much for women, though we do have an advantage: makeup."

And the right clothes, April considered. These days, she dressed not to impress Peter, but to intimidate him. Her appearance was her armor. At every face-to-face meeting, she made certain to project the aura of a successful businesswoman, worldly-wise and hardened to life's little inconveniences.

One last look in the mirror and a quick finger swipe over her teeth and she headed downstairs for today's summit.

Peter's deep laughter carried over the joyous sounds of Michael's greetings, through the foyer to the landing, where she stood for a long moment. Fisting her hands at her sides, she leaned into the archway between the stairs and the front door to get a sneak preview. He still had the same broad shoulders—God, how she'd always loved throwing her arms around those shoulders—the same wheaten hair. It was hard to believe, but he looked yummier now than he had at seventeen. Marriage to Lori must agree with him.

Or maybe he looks so good to me because it's been such a long time since I've had a man, any man, in the house.

"Hello, Peter," she said as she strode into the foyer, secretly hoping she oozed confidence.

Hazel eyes, so like Michael's but without the epicanthal fold, scanned her from head to toe in one long sweep. "Hi, April. You're looking good."

Yup, she had him trembling in his shoes now. He was just too embarrassed to show his terror in front of their son.

Dream on, April.

Probably to avoid a prolonged conversation with her, he turned to Michael. "Why don't you go get your gear?"

"Okay." Michael stampeded past her and up the stairs, sounding only slightly louder than a herd of buffalo.

April watched Michael disappear, then glanced at her former husband. "Thanks for taking him for the month."

Peter's gaze fell to the carpeting at their feet. "Yeah, well, about that . . ."

Some things never changed. She knew that sudden avoidance of eye contact, that penitent posture.

Brace yourself, April. He's about to drop a bomb on you.

"What?" she asked, her fingernails digging into her palms as she tried to keep calm. "What 'about that'?"

"There's been a change in plans," he told the carpet. "I'm only going to be able to keep him the first two weeks you're away. Lori and I are taking a cruise to Bermuda for our anniversary. We leave on the fifteenth."

"But your anniversary is two months from now."

The fifteenth was the anniversary of their divorce. Was there a hidden message in that choice of date for his trip with Lori? Her cheeks stung as if she'd been slapped.

"Right now," Peter said, "the rates are off-season. Next month, they go up."

Figures. She should have known. He was still the same old Peter—selfish, irresponsible . . . and cheap.

"Why didn't you tell me this when you insisted I do the Harmony House bit? You said it wouldn't be a problem to keep Michael for the month."

"I didn't know they'd want you so fast. And anyway, Lori's the one who booked this trip and—"

"And what? You didn't know about it when we spoke last week? She wanted to surprise you? Was she going to blindfold you, then let you guess your location when you smelled the ocean?"

"Ditch the sarcasm, will you? Look, I'm sorry. You're right. I should have told you about the trip before now, but you know how you get—"

"How *I* get?" She threw up her hands in surrender. "This is just great. Now what am I supposed to do?"

"See? This is what I mean. What's the big deal? Call that business of yours and get someone to stay with him for the last half of the month."

"Just like that?" She snapped her fingers before his face, but

Peter didn't flinch. "Do you have any idea what kind of effect that could have on him?"

"You're the one who always says we should treat him as any normal kid. Besides, don't you have a nurse on staff at that place of yours?"

"That's not the point—"

"Yes, that *is* the point. Your company can't do a favor for its owner?"

"Not with twenty-four hours' notice," she retorted.

"C'mon, April. Why do you always make things out to be so dire? You've got two weeks, not twenty-four hours."

Her eyes rolled so far back she thought she glimpsed her brain. *Same old Peter.* "*I* have twenty-four hours. By seven P.M. tomorrow, I have to be at Harmony House. The place has no phones, no computers, no mail delivery. I'll have no contact with the outside world. I can't even send a message by carrier pigeon!"

"I could call my parents if you want."

"I am *not* sending Michael to Florida for two weeks in the middle of the school year. He needs stability right now."

A reverberating shuffle from above reminded her of their son's proximity. Any minute now, he'd come downstairs. The last thing she wanted was for him to hear their quarrel. As she'd done a thousand times before, she swallowed her anger and waved her ex-husband away.

"Forget it, Peter," she said in a much softer voice. "I'll take care of the details." *As usual.*

Peter grinned. "There. Was that so hard?"

Chapter Four

The main office of Rainey-Day-Wife encompassed the first floor of a three-story building. Thanks to floor-to-ceiling windows looking out onto the street, the site projected a goldfish bowl aura. To the outside world, today hinted at another relaxing weekend, but in April's business, Saturday and Sunday were known as crunch time.

When April barged in, her assistant, Brenda, looked up from several sets of folders littering her desktop and blew a wisp of platinum blond hair out of her eyes. "April? What's up?"

Too drained to respond, April waved off Brenda's concern and headed straight for her office. Once there, she shrugged out of her jacket and hung it on the hook protruding from the wall. After stuffing her purse into the lowest drawer, she collapsed into the soft leather chair. One arm draped across the desktop, and her head sank, hiding her eyes behind her bent elbow.

"Wanna tell me what you're doing here?"

The question, not entirely unexpected, caused April to look up. Sure enough, Brenda stood in the doorway, her arms folded over her chest.

Tension drained from April's shoulders and pooled onto the carpet protector at her feet. "Making sure you've got things under control," she said with a tired smile.

"Don't lie to me. What's up? Is everything all right?"

She sighed. "No, everything's not all right. Peter pulled another fast one. He and Lori are going away on the fifteenth."

"Don't tell me." Brenda lowered her tone several octaves. " 'You work for a parenting services organization. Let them service your parenting needs. Isn't that why you're the boss?'" A smile split her apple cheeks. "Am I close?"

"Better than close. You got him spot-on."

"So you need someone to stay with the kids the last two weeks of the month?"

April nodded, suddenly too exhausted to speak.

"Give me ten minutes, and I'll see what I can come up with."

April shot up a hand, but Brenda turned toward the door before she could form a cohesive argument.

"Relax," Brenda tossed over her shoulder. "Everything's under control."

While April sat slack-jawed, Brenda slipped back into the humming melee outside.

Under control. Yeah, right. Nothing had been under control since April was a child. Her father used to call her Princess Chaos, a whirlwind of trouble in a pint-sized frame. Dad was gone now, but nothing else had changed. She still seemed to run from one firestorm into another. A wave of self-pity washed over her as she toyed with the pen and pencil desk set that had once belonged to the first man in her life. Too bad Dad hadn't lived long enough to see the success of her company. Her accomplishments might have bolstered his faith in his eldest daughter. After all the times she'd disappointed him, it would have been nice to see pride sparkling in those sherry-colored eyes—just once.

Mom, after all, was a lost cause.

Brenda rapped her knuckles on the door before walking inside and dropping a manila folder on April's desk. "All set."

"What's this?" April asked, picking up the folder.

"As an official client of Rainey-Day-Wife," Brenda said in her practiced tone, "you must fill out the enclosed paperwork regarding your child. Names and phone numbers for pediatrician and dentist, after-school activity schedules, allergies, food likes and dislikes, emergency contact information, et cetera."

"You found someone already? Who?"

"First admit I'm the best assistant you ever had."

"You're the *only* assistant I ever had."

"That's immaterial," Brenda replied, sitting down. She placed her hands on the desktop and rolled her chair closer. "Now ask me how I spent the last five minutes while you sat in here, no doubt reflecting on the unfairnesses of life."

April sighed and shook her head in mock defeat. "You're Superwoman, okay, Brenda? I couldn't survive without you. Is that what you want to hear?"

"For a start." She paused to preen, flipping her hair over one shoulder and giving a little upper-body shimmy. Within the blink of an eye, her posture straightened and she once again became the Mistress of All Things Business. "I made one simple phone call on your behalf. My mom says she'll watch Michael at your house for the last half of the month at no charge."

April rubbed her soft fingertips over her throbbing temples. This was a bad omen. Maybe she should just back out of this whole Harmony House deal. "No, Brenda. I can't ask your mom to come live at my house and stay with Michael—"

"Why not? She's watched him before."

"For a few hours, not for two whole weeks. Would she know what to do if something happened? He has special needs—"

"She worked as a rehab specialist for twenty years, April."

"Yeah, but I feel awful, strong-arming her into my mess."

"Hey, she volunteered. Ever since Dad retired, she's going out of her mind at home. Their latest running argument is whether she should dust before vacuuming or vacuum before dusting." She giggled. "Besides, Mom can't wait to see the fireworks between you and Dr. Jeff. She says that's payment enough. Well, that and the little side bet she has going with her mah-jongg club."

Despite the misgivings whispering in April's head, her curiosity sat up, and she focused one eye on Brenda. "Who's she putting her money on?"

"You, of course. She likes Dr. Jeff, but she remembers who hired her daughter when no one else would."

April smiled at the reminder. Five years earlier, she'd found Brenda and her three children huddled together in a serpentine line at the welfare office. A short conversation later, she'd hired Rainey-Day-Wife's first employee. And she'd never once regretted that decision. Brenda *was* Superwoman, handling all the administrative duties with ease.

"That was a long time ago. Now you could work anywhere."

"I don't want to work 'anywhere.' I love working here." Brenda rose. "Now, go home. You've got serious psychologist butt to kick starting tomorrow. All your problems are solved—thanks to my brilliance and my mother's generosity—so go home and get some rest."

All her problems were solved? Why, then, did she believe they'd only begun?

Rest did not come easy for April. Not only because her nerves kept her fidgeting around her quiet, empty house, but because her sister Summer decided to call to wish her luck. *Luck. Ha.*

"Listen, Sum," she said after the usual pleasantries. "Can I call you later? I'm in the middle of something here—"

"Packing for your month with the yummy doctor, I bet," Summer said. "God, I can't believe how lucky you are. Imagine! Getting the chance to *live* with that scrumptious specimen for a whole month. I'd leave Brad in a heartbeat for such an opportunity." In a quick whisper, she added, "But don't tell him I said that."

April sighed. Of course not. Brad, the perfect husband, would keel over if he knew that his perfect wife had a crush on a television star.

"Anyway," her sister continued, "that's the reason I called. I wanted to make sure you weren't going to make *another* huge mistake. Like you did on the show."

"What did I do on the show?"

"You came off pretty snotty, don't you think? I mean, right from the get-go with that bit about everyone looking for a mommy. But when you confronted Dr. Jeff . . . oh my God, I thought I'd have a heart attack and drop dead right there in my living room."

That would never happen. Not in Summer's perfect, should-be-roped-off-like-a-museum living room. Her falling body might crush the carpet nap.

Not nice. April's conscience chastised her, and she bit her tongue to keep the retort in check. "I was nervous on the show. I blurt things out when I'm nervous."

Summer's lighthearted giggle skittered down April's spinal cord like ice cubes. "Yeah, exactly like Dad. You got two things from him—your business acumen and that tendency toward sarcasm."

Lord, if she bit her tongue any harder, she might cut it in half. "Is there a point to any of this?"

"Of course there's a point. I was thinking . . ." Summer took a deep breath.

April tensed. *Uh-oh. Here we go.*

"When you get to Harmony House tomorrow, take the opportunity to atone to Dr. Jeff for your rudeness. Be nice. Show him you're not the hard-hearted witch you came off as. Mom and I already talked about this, and we believe it's the right thing to do."

"You talked to Mom about my appearance on the show and what I should do?" The very idea kinked her stomach into greasy knots.

"Not that you'll listen." Summer's voice reclaimed its position as her older sister's conscience. "I mean, just think how much better off you'd have been if you'd listened to Mom and Dad back in high school."

April nearly dropped the phone. "For God's sake, that was almost twenty years ago."

"Mom told you not to marry Peter, but would you listen? Of course not. Don't get me wrong; I love Becky. But you would have been so much better off if you'd taken Mom's advice, given the baby up for adoption, and finished high school. You could have gone on to college, found a decent career, and you wouldn't be in the boat you're in now. . . ."

Summer's scolding, practiced and familiar, fragmented into a thousand nonsensical syllables as April cast a glance at the photo on the fridge of a pretty young woman in a gold-and-green graduate's cap and gown. Beside Becky's photo was Michael's, his sweet deer eyes sparkling with the magic of innocence.

Warmth flooded her heart. Her children could transform the most miserable day into myriad moments of agony, joy, love, and pride. And she'd do anything to keep them safe, happy, and cared for.

Determination stiffened her spine as she gripped the phone tighter. "Sorry, but I'm going to have to disappoint you and Mom. *Again.* I'm playing to win."

Before Summer could argue, April hung up and quickly turned off the ringer to avoid any additional debate.

Chapter Five

The following day, April sat wedged against the door in the limousine, as far away from her companion as possible. She didn't dare look at Dr. Jeff, instead focusing on the turnpike outside the tinted window. Every white line whizzing past brought her that much closer to the site of her self-imposed monthlong imprisonment. Why, oh, why had she consented to this?

Conversations she'd had with various friends and family members echoed in her head, forming a mishmash of sound bites.

"Go for it, April," Brenda had urged. "Show the world Dr. Jeff is a quack, and I guarantee no one will ever take him seriously again. Besides, Deirdre and I can handle things here for a month. It'll be good practice for when we open the satellite office in Queens next year."

Her daughter, Becky, had been all for the experiment, secure in the knowledge her mom could hold her own. "Dr. Jeff goes around spouting this crap about how women have lost control of their lives by trying to have a family *and* a career. If anyone can show him how it's done, it's you, Mom."

April supposed she should be grateful her daughter had so much confidence in her.

Not to be outdone, Peter had thrown in his two cents. "You need this opportunity. *We* need this opportunity. For Michael. There's going to come a time when we'll have to think about long-term care for him. If you win this Harmony House thing, you'll not only get a little added exposure for your company, you'll win enough money to keep him comfortable for a long time. What could be better?"

"Dining with swine comes to mind."

"Not funny." Even over the phone, his disapproval diminished her spirit. Peter had never understood her sense of humor.

"Look, Peter, this challenge is no picnic. A full month? Living with that coldhearted weasel?"

"He won't be so coldhearted if he's trying to woo you with 'infinite acts of love and consideration.' You can do this, April."

Naturally, dear old Mom saw this as another opening to remind April how much she'd screwed up her life. "I just hope you're not making another mistake."

Okay, so marrying before she'd finished high school might not have been her smartest move. But she'd never thought twice about keeping her daughter, or Michael, for that matter, even when the severity of his condition became apparent. Shoot, she wouldn't trade Michael for the healthiest boy on earth.

These were her kids, her lifeblood, the reason she got up in the morning. Most important, they were the reason she sat in this limousine now, Dr. Jeff a few feet away, en route to an isolated cabin in the Adirondacks where she'd remain for thirty days, playing house with a perfect stranger.

No, this was not perfect. Far from it.

She stole a glance in Dr. Jeff's direction. Heat infused her cheeks when her eyes locked on his. Why was he staring at her? What was he thinking?

Jeff's eyes might have been on Ms. Raine, but his thoughts were miles away.

Who was to blame for his current predicament? Rodney, his termite of an agent, who couldn't find a loophole in his ironclad contract with the network to wriggle him out? David Darwin, the executive producer of *Taking Sides,* who'd come up with this boneheaded scheme to begin with? Ms. Raine, who couldn't resist her fifteen minutes of fame and the chance to win a hundred thousand dollars?

No. He had no one to blame but himself. Not that the admission did anything to soothe his current frustration. Placing blame didn't solve anything. If it did, he'd be as placid as the Dalai Lama by now.

Back at Harvard, his sociology professor had advised him, "No one comes into your life without a purpose. Each person you meet, no matter how briefly, is sent to teach you or be taught by you."

Jeff had met Emma around the same time he'd scoffed at his professor's sagacity. Only after she was gone did he understand the truth behind those words.

Now a single thread ran through the fabric of his days: *Never take those you love for granted. Every moment together is an opportunity to remind them how much they're valued.*

To atone for his transgressions, he'd devoted his practice to this new credo, written a best-selling book on the subject, and appeared on the talk show circuit. Then his agent's idea for a list of the Most Family-Unfriendly Businesses in New York came along. He'd foolishly fallen for the bait and the subsequent publicity tied to it, which culminated in this challenge, because April Raine saw dollar signs.

Well, he'd teach her a thing or two, mainly about where her priorities should lie. Family should always come before cash.

He'd signed on with *Taking Sides* only as a way to get his message across: that what was sorely lacking in today's hectic, sometimes violent world was simple consideration. If he could find another way to prove that—to a nationwide audience, to himself, and even to Emma's spirit—without resorting to this ridiculous challenge, he'd order the driver to pull the car over, and he'd walk away and never look back.

But no matter where he let his mind wander or what bizarre ideas he entertained, one undeniable fact continued to stare him in the face. The implacable Ms. Raine had become the only barrier standing between him and the peace he'd sought since a sunny day in August 2004 when a grim-faced obstetrician had pulled him out of the delivery room.

All he had to do was treat Ms. Raine kindly, prove to her and the television audience that *any* relationship benefitted from infinite acts of love and consideration. Then, thirty days from now, he'd be a free man, free from the doubts that had plagued him night and day since Emma died.

It was simple, really. . . .

April stepped out of the car and closed the door just hard enough to make a click. Her prison—where she'd serve her thirty-day sentence on the charge of stupidity—was an A-frame chalet. She had become a prisoner of war—a war dreamed up by a bunch of network executives, but fought by her and Dr. Jefferson Prentiss.

Thirty-five years old and I've been drafted.

Her shaking legs carried her toward a jag where the land fell away. A chilly breeze surged, whipping her unzipped jacket so that it looked like the wings of a bird taking flight. She shivered as the wind's fingers reached through her cable-knit sweater, causing goose bumps on her skin. *Dang!* She'd forgotten how cold it could be up here.

While she fumbled with the zipper's tab, clean mountain air filled her nostrils. A hint of smoke lingered, and sooty clouds, wafting from a brick chimney, floated across the chambray sky.

Harmony House, a modern yet rustic home, fit its location as well as its title. The site offered no glimpses of civilization. April hadn't seen a storefront or a building of any kind since they'd exited the Northway twenty minutes back.

Pristine silence reigned but for a nearby stream's muted gurgle. Nature's serenity enveloped her, calmed her, and soothed the nervous tremors she'd suffered on the long drive here.

"Nice view."

That smooth voice, tinged with humor, broke the stillness around and inside her.

The air hummed with anticipation—or frayed nerve endings tingled in her ears. She couldn't tell which. Every sense jumped to full alert and her heartbeat increased to a rock-and-roll tempo. Why did this guy affect her so?

Her flesh had tightened again, beginning around the muscles of her lower jaw and moving downward. She suddenly felt like a deer caught in an oncoming vehicle's path—knowing the looming danger, yet helpless to avoid the collision.

"Ready to see where we'll be imprisoned for the next month?"

Despite the paralysis still holding her from the neck down, she couldn't help smiling. Hadn't she compared this little house to a prison? At least they had *one* thing in common.

"What's that old song?" She sang the line she remembered from a Tweety Bird cartoon. " 'I'm only a bird in a gilded cage . . . ' "

He laughed. It was a rich, throaty sound. "Come on." He took her arm in a loose grasp. "Let's go inside."

April stole one last look at the sun, light paling as dusk gobbled up the sky bite by bite. Along with it went her freedom. With a deep sigh, partly of regret and partly of irritation, she followed Dr. Jeff through the front door and met chaos head-on.

Men and women scurried everywhere in the living room, shouting orders to one another. Boom mikes hung from exposed rafters. Ladders, secured to the floor of the loft, allowed the lighting crew to adjust spots mounted near the thirty-foot ceiling. Thick cables littered the hardwood floor and handwoven area rug, creating a giant obstacle course of black snakes.

"May I?" Dr. Jeff stood over her, his hands on her shoulders.

"May you what?" The tornado of activity around her commanded her full attention.

"Your coat," he said. "I'll take your coat."

She shook off whatever stupor had overtaken her, and mumbled, "Thanks." After unzipping her jacket, she allowed him to remove it from her shoulders.

She waited while Dr. Jeff hung her jacket along with his expensive-looking wool coat in a closet by the door.

A smiling young man bounded toward them, his hand extended in welcome. "Oh, terrific. You guys are here. Doctor, good to see you again." Jeff shook the man's hand. "Your timing couldn't be better. You must be Ms. Raine. I'm David Darwin, executive producer of *Taking Sides*. I'll be in charge of the competition."

Executive producer? He barely looked old enough to have graduated high school. "Please, call me April," she replied, shaking his hand.

"It's a pleasure to meet you, April. Wow, your hands are cold. Why don't you two go warm up by the fire while I have someone bring your things inside?" He turned to shout at a burly man near one of the ladders. "Tony? You wanna help the driver with the luggage, please?"

The youthful exuberance in his tone reminded April of Becky and her friends. Perhaps because of that kindling of memory, he shot straight up on her approval scale.

"You got it, Dave," the man replied in a voice that boomed deep enough to shake the rafters.

With Tony gone, David returned his attention to April and Jeff. "There's coffee and pastries in the kitchen, if you're interested. When you're ready to get under way, start going through the pantry and decide what kind of groceries you'll need for the next week. Get a list together so Maggie can do the food shopping before the stores close."

Halfway toward the welcoming fire, April stopped at David's last instruction. "Can't we shop for ourselves?"

"No," he replied. "Once you're here, you're here for the duration. You won't be allowed to leave for any reason—except an emergency, of course. Whatever you need will be brought in for you by staff members."

" 'I'm only a bird in a gilded cage . . . ' "

April gasped as shivers ratcheted up her spine. Jeff was singing in her ear, his warm breath dancing across her nape.

She whispered the next line: " 'A beautiful sight to see.' "

He burst out laughing, and she joined him, enjoying the break in their impasse.

David obviously didn't get the joke. He cleared his throat, his expression showing disapproval. "Once things quiet down, I'll take you on a tour of the house. Then we'll go over the shooting schedules and what you can expect during the next thirty days. Sound good to you?"

Jeff nodded. "Yes. Thanks, David."

David clapped and then rubbed his hands together like a child promised ice cream. "Great. In the meantime, I'll make sure Tony's taken all of your things to the bedroom."

Wait a minute.

The breath left April's lungs. "I think Dr. Jeff and I would like to choose our own rooms." She turned to Dr. Jeff, beside her. "Isn't that right?"

David's gaze slipped from one to the other, his brow puckering with anxiety. "Oh, but there is no choice. Harmony House only has one bedroom."

Chapter Six

If someone had pitched the room into darkness, April couldn't have been more surprised—or terrified.

"What do you mean there's only one bedroom?"

"Just what I said." David shrugged. "Usually the place is used for marital counseling, one couple at a time. The professionals in charge insisted on only one bedroom in Harmony House. Supposedly, proximity encourages togetherness."

"What about couples who *aren't* married?" Dr. Jeff demanded.

David shrugged again. "Beats me. You're the first such couple. You'll have to wing it, I guess."

Wing it? Was he kidding? April sputtered but couldn't form a single coherent word. To think that only a moment earlier, she'd considered him a nice guy . . .

Now what? Was it too late to turn around and get out of here? What other surprises did Harmony House have in store?

Claustrophobia held her in a tight grip. The need to escape overwhelmed her, but her feet refused to move.

"Is there a reason the production team didn't share this information with Ms. Raine or me before we arrived here today?" Dr. Jeff's growl brought her attention back to the farce unfolding before her.

David's shoulders moved again, but Dr. Jeff cut him off in mid-stroke. "Don't shrug at me like a helpless idiot. I'm sure you were in on this, David. You knew the network set us up. You knew we wouldn't be happy with the sleeping arrangements. So what's the deal? Was this supposed to be our first episode? Filming our outraged reactions?"

"Well, er, uh . . ." David looked at his feet.

The producer's sudden avoidance confirmed April's worst fear—that *Taking Sides* planned to make a fool of her with this experiment. "Oh my God. David, is this true?"

"Of course it's true," Dr. Jeff replied. "These manipulative creeps planned to catch our surprise and outrage on tape for tomorrow morning's audience."

"Is that true, David?" She knew she was repeating herself, but her brain refused to accept what her ears heard. She couldn't fathom such a Machiavellian plan.

"Now, April," David finally said, "it's not as bad as you think. . . ."

"In other words, yes," she snapped, and turned toward Dr. Jeff. "Get my coat, please. I'm leaving."

David shook his head. "I wouldn't do that if I were you."

"Oh? Why not?"

"Because you'd be opening yourself up to a hefty lawsuit for breach of contract."

Her anger deflated, leaving panic to fill her senses. That mountain of paperwork she'd signed and initialed when agreeing to this disaster! She'd lose everything if they sued her.

Then where would Michael be? In some cruel institution? She shivered.

Jeff leaned over her. "They have a battery of lawyers who *live* for this kind of thing," he whispered. "Don't give them the satisfaction. Accept it, and I promise we'll work something out when David's gone."

"So . . . ?" The youthfulness of David's voice reminded her of elementary school bullies. Even his posture, arms folded over his chest, weight balanced on one hip, screamed *arrogance*. "What's it going to be, April?"

Surrender sapped her. What else could she do? Was her pride worth the possibility of losing her house, her company? Michael?

Squelching a cringe, April forced a smile, tightening every facial muscle in the process. "Make sure Tony doesn't leave any of my luggage outside."

"Very wise," David replied, then turned and left them alone.

She and the doctor stood in the foyer, two lost sheep, afraid to look at anything or anyone. Despite the ongoing noise of power tools and workmen, silence became a wall between them.

At last, Dr. Jeff broke the disquiet. "Are you hungry?"

"No." While what little logic was functioning in her brain appreciated his deft subject change, her stomach refused to put in an appearance at this meeting. Food held no interest with that single-bedroom issue looming over her.

"Me neither," he said. "Come on. Let me get you a cup of coffee while we try to figure out some kind of solution."

"Sounds good." Maybe she could drink gallons of the stuff and stay awake for the next thirty days. Then she wouldn't have to worry about where she slept.

They sidestepped electrical cords, utility ladders, and men who carried production equipment she couldn't lift or name if she tried. As it often did in dark moments, her sense of humor kicked in.

Where would they hang the WELCOME TO PURGATORY sign? Probably in the bedroom she and Dr. Jeff were supposed to inhabit.

Panic seized her again. Seeking some form of escape, she flicked her eyes to the window and the couch beneath it, an open-armed contraption of rough-hewn oak and hideous lumpy plaid.

One of us will have to sleep on that medieval torture device, because I'm not sharing a bed with a complete stranger. She shot a look at the good doctor. *And guess whose back is about to suffer.*

Apparently unaware of the way her thoughts had turned, Dr. Jeff smiled. She offered him a wishy-washy grin in return.

He then pointed to three high stools tucked underneath a long counter, which formed a breakfast nook, separating the kitchen from the dining area. "Have a seat, and I'll get us a couple of coffees."

A stainless steel urn sat in the corner, surrounded by Styrofoam cups, milk, a rainbow of sugar and artificial-sweetener packets, stirrers, and napkins. An oblong basket of Danish waited nearby, filling the air with a sweet, oily odor.

While he fussed with the cups and the urn's tap, she took a

moment to size up the rest of the kitchen. A gourmet chef's dream, it housed a six-burner stove with a double oven, rich cherry cabinetry, marble countertops, a cherry worktable with built-in shelves, and a walk-in pantry set among the usual culinary necessities. Behind her, a cherry dining room table and six matching chairs sat ready for use.

What deranged architect had designed this place? Only one bedroom, but a kitchen that could easily provide dinner for an entire high school?

Then again, when you can't leave the house for a month at a time, what else is there to do but eat and . . .

Thinking of the second alternative made steam rise in her neck and cheeks. To cool the burn, she jerked her gaze from the expansive kitchen to its lone occupant. Dr. Jeff's thick, dark hair was a trifle long, skimming the edge of his collar. His smooth skin and easy smile gave him a down-to-earth look, not at all the scholarly mien she would have expected from a PhD with his educational credits. Didn't Harvard grads all look like bookworms with slicked hair, nerd glasses, and pocket protectors?

Well, Dr. Jeff completely shattered that image from head to toe. The shirt he wore was a little too bulky for her to get a good look at his upper body, but from what she could discern, the guy had a physique like granite. Curious, she noted the width of his back.

I'll bet he does push-ups. You don't get shoulders that broad by writing notes on a pad all day, that's for sure.

"How do you take yours?"

Jeff's question shook her back to her senses. *Oh, God.* Had he noticed her ogling him?

"I-I'm sorry. What?"

"Your coffee?" he asked, lifting the white cup in his hand.

If he saw anything lascivious in her face, his curious expression gave no indication. What made her start considering his physique? This wasn't a tryst, for goodness sake.

Jeff was the enemy. Well, sort of. *Taking Sides* expected him to win her over. And here she stood, mentally falling for his looks, analyzing his musculature, making his job that much easier.

"Milk, no sugar," she managed to reply as she sank into one of the stools he'd designated earlier.

He joined her there, placing one coffee before her and setting another down on the counter. She noted he took his black. What did that say about him? Did a hidden meaning lurk in the way a person drank his coffee, just as, some proclaimed, sleep positions, zodiac signs, or invisible auras indicated one's personality?

"I'm glad you decided to stay," he said, but his expression lacked any evidence of happiness. His brow furrowed and his eyebrows knitted tightly together as he stared into the contents of the white foam cup.

"Would they really have sued me if I'd walked out?"

"You'd better believe it. My guess is the producers sold a lot of advertising time based on our upcoming appearances on *Taking Sides* every day. If you were to pull out now and the show went down the tubes, who would reimburse the sponsors? Not the network, that's for sure. They'd come after you and me to recoup their losses."

"But that's not fair."

"Who said television is fair? Let me tell you something, Ms. Raine—"

"April," she said, automatically correcting him.

"April," he repeated, a bitter smile crossing his features. "And I'm Jeff. No sense standing on formalities at this stage, is there?" She shook her head. "Well, let me explain something about the wonderful world of television. Most people thought reality shows would have crashed and burned by now. But they're still a big draw for the networks, even though there's no reality in them."

"I don't follow you," she said as she sipped the hot brew. It tasted ghastly, but at least it warmed her insides.

"People don't want reality; they want the illusion of reality. In a world where computers do all our communicating, we're reaching farther, but becoming less connected to those closest to us."

"And you think television is trying to fill that void?"

"In a way. Reality television gives people a chance to bond with a stranger on some level, usually by way of common foibles. The networks are taking advantage of that desire for simpler times, days when you knew your neighbors and everything about them. The reality show is a window into the lives of others. We've become a nation of voyeurs, living vicariously through someone else's exploits without leaving the comfort of our own living rooms."

"So people can fool themselves into thinking they're in touch with reality when they're not?"

"Precisely."

She tilted her head, studied his face for any hint of humor in his expression. She found none. "That's awfully cynical."

"No, it's fact. Television is an illusion, all glittering clothes and glamorous faces. No substance. It's a lot like Snow White's apple. From the outside, it looks perfect, ripe, and beautiful. Such a temptation. But on the inside, it's poison."

Was he trying to frighten her off, after he'd just said he was glad she'd stayed?

Her fingertips brushed his dry palm, and electricity passed between them. The sensation jolted tingles from her nails to her wrist. But she didn't pull away. She couldn't.

His hypnotic eyes held her, inhibiting the slightest motion. A longing rose within her, to be embraced, to dance with someone, to bend as a man dipped her low, low, lower still. Debilitating heat burned her insides until her mouth dried to the moisture level of Sahara sand. Each inhalation of breath sapped more strength. Her heart pounded. Meanwhile, her veins pulsed to some inner rhythm, keeping the tempo of a punk rock ballad.

When he leaned closer, her back arched—and she nearly toppled off the stool for her trouble.

What was wrong with her? They'd been together for only a few hours, and already visions of champagne, moonlight, and slow, deep kisses filled the movie screen in her head.

"Don't lose your soul, April. No television show or career goal is worth that price."

His fluid voice splashed over her skin, carrying her back to reality in a riptide. The tension she'd noted earlier eased. All the furrows and lines in his face had disappeared.

Did he expect a reply? To what? What had he last said? Something about not losing her soul?

"I— I won't," she managed to say.

Jeff took a sip of coffee and grimaced. "Blech. Must be the bottom of the pot. This tastes like transmission fluid." He placed the cup down on the counter. "Whaddya say we check out the bedroom and find a solution to our current dilemma?"

Right now, her legs wouldn't support her if she tried to climb off the stool. "What about the pantry? Shouldn't we make a shopping list first?"

He waved her off. "Don't let David's warnings about store closings faze you too much. It's still early. The local supermarket should be open for at least another two hours. Are you ready?"

She took one last sip of coffee, hoping to swallow some bit of fortitude along with the caffeine, but her mouth automatically pursed in reaction. Jeff was right. The acidic taste did more harm than good to her nervous stomach.

"I'm as ready as I'll ever be," she replied, and slid off the stool onto rubbery legs.

Chapter Seven

*O*h, *this just keeps getting better all the time. . . .*

Jeff stared at the four-poster bed, the Laura Ashley fripperies, the glass-enclosed fireplace, the crystal dishes of potpourri, and the array of pillared candles. He cringed. Who had decorated this place? Victoria's Secret?

A quick glance at April told him she was just as uncomfortable with the sumptuously romantic theme displayed here. Her lips had disappeared inside a tight line, and her complexion paled to chalk white.

"Oh, God." She turned away in embarrassment—or shame.

He couldn't tell which, and it really didn't matter. The same muddled emotions tumbled around his brain.

"I think I'll sleep in the living room," he said, hoping he conveyed a lighthearted air in contrast to his thoughts.

April's attention returned to the king-sized bed. "I don't think it'll be necessary," she murmured. "I have a better idea. Have you ever seen the movie *It Happened One Night*?"

"Isn't that the Christmas one with a bunch of ghosts?"

For a moment he caught the whites of her eyes before she refocused on him with a look of pure exasperation. "No, it was a 1930s movie with Clark Gable and Claudette Colbert. You see, she's an heiress who's married to a guy her father disapproves of. When Daddy imprisons her on his yacht, she escapes to return to her husband. But she winds up hooking up with a reporter—that's Clark Gable—and he agrees to take her to New York in exchange for exclusive rights to her story."

The synopsis flew from her lips at a rapid pace, and he blinked several times, trying to absorb the information. He had no luck.

"Well, on their way to New York, they pretend to be a married couple, but that gets dicey when they have to spend the night in a hotel. But of course, she's already married, so for modesty's sake, they string up a blanket, separating the double beds, which the Clark Gable character starts calling the Walls of Jericho."

Where exactly was she headed with this movie review? What did this have to do with—

Tink! A lightbulb flared in his brain.

"Wait a minute. Are you suggesting we string up a blanket to separate the two sections of the bed?"

Her smile bordered on smug. "Why not?"

Why not? Was she kidding? "Because you're missing one very important prop from that movie. In those days, the hero and heroine slept in separate beds."

She said nothing at first; she merely walked around the bed as if studying it from every angle. "I've made a lot of beds in my time, first as a maid for an oceanfront time-share and then at Rainey-Day-Wife. Now, I might be wrong"—she reached for the corner of the splashy coverlet—"but I'll bet . . ." She flipped the covers up and tossed her hand in the air with the finesse of a spokesmodel at a car show. "Voila!"

He studied the bed with interest. A deep crease ran through the center of it. *What the . . . ?* Returning his gaze to her, he asked, "Twin mattresses?"

She beamed. "Mmm-hmm. They're actually a little shorter than a king-sized mattress. The frame hooks them together, and the blankets make the bed look larger. The worst part is actually sleeping on this the way it is. One partner always winds up sleeping in the crack."

Anything beat sleeping on that wooden rack in the living room. Relief flooded through his veins. "Well, something tells me we won't have that problem."

"That's for sure. Why don't we unpack, then have David bring someone in here to separate the headboard from the beds?" She pointed to a dresser with a trifold mirror. "I'll take that one. You can have the armoire on the other side."

April felt a little more relaxed now, after having solved the issue of the sleeping situation so handily. After lifting her suitcase onto the bed and unlocking it, she flipped open the lid. If she could hide her suddenly hot face, she would. Assigning him the armoire in what might have come across as an imperious manner probably smacked of bossiness to his psychological mind. In reality, it was little more than a ruse to keep his back to her. His proximity still made her antsy.

April quickly removed her underwear from her suitcase and shoved it into the first available drawer. She might not want him looking at her face, but she definitely didn't want him sneaking a peek at her lacy unmentionables—or the pretty pink case that housed her secret pick-me-up equipment buried beneath her sweaters.

"You surprise me."

"I do?" April's gaze snapped up from her colorful array of sweaters and jeans to meet Jeff's.

That was a big mistake. Those soulful eyes reflected a genuine appreciation she wasn't accustomed to seeing from a man— any man.

"Yes, you do. You're smarter than you give yourself credit for."

"Gee, thanks." She snorted.

He started to explain, and she held up a hand.

"Don't worry. I won't let it go to my head. Besides, I'm not really book smart. I'm more like *TV Guide*–crossword-puzzle smart."

He laughed, and for the first time since they'd met, she relaxed in his presence. At least *he* appreciated her sense of humor. Maybe he wasn't such a bad guy after all.

"Nothing fazes you." He sat on the edge of the bed. "You roll with the punches and even manage to get in an uppercut or two of your own every once in a while."

She shrugged. "Oh, well, I got plenty of practice, sparring with my ex-husband."

"Care to talk about that?"

"No," she answered quickly.

"Why not?" He'd finished unpacking his belongings and now closed the suitcase with a loud zip. "I won't analyze you if that's what you're afraid of. I just think we should start getting to know each other. Don't forget, we're going to be stuck together for a whole month."

"Okay." She grinned and nodded in his direction. "Then you go first."

"Me?"

"Yeah. Tell me about your wife."

"There's not much to tell."

"Sure there is. Every marriage has stories."

The expression on his face changed from interested to stricken. Sympathy rolled over her in waves. The mere mention of his wife decimated the poor man. Six years after her death, Jeff obviously still had very strong feelings for her.

Those cloudy emotions forced April to face a depressing thought. If she were to die tomorrow, would anyone mourn her with such grief? Becky, of course. Michael maybe. But his mind was so often mired in the present, six months from now he'd have forgotten she'd ever existed. Besides, her kids didn't count in this scenario. Would any grown man miss her? Really miss her?

Probably not. The realization crushed her, and she sank onto the bed.

"You know," she said in a much softer tone, "I remember when I heard about your wife's death. The tabloids were ruthless, especially the *Inquisitor.* All that speculation and innuendo. As if your wife really was the evil villainess she played on *Tomorrow Is Another Day.* I don't know how you managed to get past all that. If it were me, I probably would have sued them."

Stony silence greeted her remarks. Had she overstepped her boundaries? After all, they were still strangers. Who was she to judge what he did about his wife's portrayal in the media?

Just when she thought he'd never answer, his morose sigh pierced the air.

"Sometimes the easiest way to breathe life into an idle rumor is to challenge it." Eyes steely, he rose, his posture ramrod straight. "If you'll excuse me, I think I'll go back to the kitchen and start our shopping list for Maggie."

She would have bitten her tongue, but she'd already stuck her foot in her mouth.

Good going, April. Remind him of his wife's death and question how he handled the press. Why don't you go the extra mile and kick him in the chops while you're at it?

"Jeff, wait. I'm sorry."

It was too little too late. He disappeared from the room as the door closed behind him.

Yessiree, this is going to be one fun-filled month. . . .

Jeff called on some inner font of Herculean strength to move his leaden feet down the hallway. Under normal circumstances, he probably would have sued that *Inquisitor.* Unfortunately, the details of Emma's death weren't normal. And the article they'd printed resembled the truth too closely.

Of course, no reputable paper had picked up the story, and the scandal had dissolved without a solid lead. Still, as usual, the mention of his late wife's name brought too many images flashing across his brain, images he hated to face, despite the passage of time.

"Hey, Doc!" David's shout came at the right time. Jeff welcomed the interruption—any interruption, even from David. "Wow, that's some firecracker we've tied you to, eh?"

"April?" Jeff looked back at the closed door to the bedroom and frowned. She'd no doubt demand an excuse for his odd behavior later. "Well, she'll certainly make the next thirty days interesting."

"I'll bet." David nudged him in the ribs.

Jeff stepped out of nudge reach and glowered. "Watch it, David. She's a lady."

"Oh, yeah? How do you know? Did you put the moves on her back there, and she turned you down?"

"How old are you?"

Splotches of color spattered David's peach-fuzz cheeks. "I'm not too old to try. What's with you? You're living with a woman who must have some kind of Viking blood in her veins. I mean, come on! You're sharing a bedroom with her! For thirty days. Are you telling me you don't intend to even try to get something started between the two of you?"

"That's none of your business. And by the way . . ." Briefly, he explained the changes he and April wanted in their sleeping accommodations.

David smirked. "Your choice, Doc. But I think you're making a mistake."

"Just do it," Jeff ordered, and walked to the kitchen. He opened the pantry and surveyed its black emptiness with a frown. If he could crawl inside and close the door, blocking him from the seeing eyes of all those hidden cameras, he would. April presented a real problem, a problem he refused to discuss with her or David or anyone else here.

The moment they'd walked into this house together, she'd become another person. Oh, she still had that tough-as-nails exterior, but he'd already noticed moments where her actions and speech hinted at a softer, more empathetic version of the woman he'd met on the set of *Taking Sides*.

What had David called her? A Viking? A pretty good analogy. He could almost picture her as a lady warrior—horned helmet, metal breastplates, a spear she'd use to pierce a man's heart and yank it out of his chest, given half a chance. Then her pillaging side would slumber while the wide-eyed kitten who had appeared in the bedroom only moments earlier would play with her victim as if he were a dead mouse.

TV Guide–crossword-puzzle smart. Yeah, right. Over the years he'd known plenty of people who feigned humility so others would fawn over them. Emma had *mastered* that art. But in April, he sensed no wily manipulation to gain compliments.

He winced the minute the thought popped into his head.

That was his problem. He kept mentally comparing April to Emma. He felt disloyal, as if his thoughts betrayed his late wife's memory. Yet he couldn't stop the divergences from stacking up like a giant checklist in his head.

April was shorter than Emma, but more curvaceous. Whereas Emma's figure had leaned toward coltish, long and slender, April's was all woman—sinuous, soft, and sexy as all get out.

April had a marvelous sense of humor; she was feistier than Emma had ever been. Look at how she'd come up with her own business, Rainey-Day-Wife. God, even the company's name was clever. If Emma had found herself abandoned and flat broke, could she have survived and flourished the way April had?

Probably not, he suspected, and another twinge of guilt pricked him for such a traitorous thought. No doubt about it. April was Emma's direct opposite. Worse, time and again April came out on top in this contest.

"I'm sorry." Her voice came from behind him.

He whirled, smacking his head on the pantry shelf. Was that Emma's way of getting back at him?

"I didn't mean to upset you," April continued.

"You didn't upset me," he lied, resisting the urge to rub a hand along his stinging scalp. "I merely wanted to get a jump on the shopping list for Maggie."

"If you say so," she said with a shrug. "What have you come up with so far?"

Nothing. He hadn't even thought about the shopping list. But he refused to admit it. "The basics. Eggs, bread, salt and pepper."

"Where's your list?"

"Well . . ." He ducked his head inside the pantry, hoping to hide his embarrassment. "I haven't written anything down yet."

"All right." She pulled up one of the stools and sat, then reached for a pencil from a cup in the corner. "How about if you tell me what we need, and I write the list?"

"Fine. We'll start with the stuff I mentioned. Eggs, bread, salt and pepper. What about breakfast? Do you eat cereal?"

She smiled. "When I remember to eat, I usually have a yogurt and some orange juice. But I'm putting coffee on the list. I can't function without it."

He couldn't help smiling back. "That's something we have in common." And another departure from Emma, who'd only drunk tea—Earl Grey.

"Let's make it something expensive," she said as she wrote. "Kona blend. Give the producers a little payback for their game with the single bedroom."

Why couldn't Emma have been more like April?

An invisible fist punched him in the stomach seconds after the thought popped into his mind.

Chapter Eight

When they returned to the bedroom a while later, the mattresses sat on opposite sides of the room. Gone were the candles, the lace and flowery fabrics, and, best of all, the romantic atmosphere. In their place stood the two beds on frames with no headboards. The tall armoire, where he'd stored his garments, and the triple dresser with the mirror she'd used now sat kitty-corner to the beds. The place resembled a dorm room.

Or at least, Becky's dorm room. April, of course, had no personal experience with college life.

Her gaze scanned the two beds before she turned to Jeff. "Do you have a preference?"

His forehead puckered. "A preference?"

"Which bed or which side of the room?"

"No. Doesn't matter to me."

Ever since she'd mentioned his wife, except for their exchange about coffee, his demeanor had become terse, as if someone had thrown a bucket of ice water on the warm, smiling man from earlier.

Well, what do you expect, idiot? You're the one who brought up his poor wife. He probably thinks you'll poke fun at his dead grandmother next. Of all the dim-witted things to do . . .

Clearly, she'd have to break this impasse. "Do you mind if I take the bed closer to the bathroom?"

"Fine."

Terrific. A monosyllabic answer. Idle chitchat was getting her nowhere. She'd have to extend the full-fledged apology to smooth his ruffled feathers.

"Jeff, I'm really sorry about what I said before."

"What you said?"

He sure didn't believe in making it easy on her, did he? Okay, so she'd have to go full throttle. On a deep breath, she rushed through her explanation. "About your wife. I was out of line, and I'm sorry."

"You didn't say anything wrong, April."

She blinked. "I didn't?"

"No." His sigh enveloped her in sorrow. "I suppose I should be the one to apologize. I've been a little distracted, but it has nothing to do with you."

He never looked her in the eye when he made this confession, and she didn't know whether to believe him or not.

For now, she'd have to let whatever bothered him roll off her. A pile of linens lay at the foot of her mattress, and another pile of items sat on the floor. Each bundle required attention.

Start with the ones on the floor, then deal with the ones on the bed. Later we'll have to do something about the man glowering at you from across the room.

Feigning indifference to his continued stare, she picked up a length of rope and the hammer and nails she'd ordered Tony to leave behind when he'd separated the beds. After climbing onto her chosen mattress, she surveyed the room for the best location for a makeshift wall.

"What are you doing now?" Jeff's voice held a tinge of annoyance mixed with curiosity.

"I'm building our wall of Jericho. Feel like lending me a hand?"

"Why not?"

Gee, don't sound so enthused, pal.

She bit back the caustic reply and handed him one end of the clothesline. "Here, take this, and head over by that window."

He looked at the frayed end. "Where did you get the rope?"

"From the utility cabinet. It's a clothesline."

After taking a nail from her pocket, she pounded the end of the clothesline into the wall above her bed. Leaning back, she surveyed her handiwork and yanked on the end of the rope to be certain it stayed in place. Satisfied, she tossed the hammer on the bed, then stepped off and landed on the floor.

"Your turn." She walked toward his side of the room with the hammer and another nail in her hand. "Nail the line in on your side, but make sure it's good and taut. Once we drape the sheets over, it's bound to sag due to the excess weight."

His eyebrows rose. "Were you a Girl Scout, by chance?"

"No." It was an odd question. "Why?"

"I've just never met someone as resourceful as you."

A heated blush traveled across her cheeks. "Yes, well," she replied, "desperation is the mother of invention."

"I thought necessity was the mother."

She shrugged. "Same thing."

By nine o'clock, the last of the production crew finished their work and exited the house. Even David said good night, but not before announcing he'd return at seven A.M. sharp to get the two residents ready for their first on-air appearance.

After the door closed, April sat with Jeff in the living room. The mood in the room grew uncomfortably heavy. Mentally, she compared the feeling to that of being stuck in an elevator with a stranger. Unfortunately, she didn't even have annoying Muzak to break the silence. That invisible wall rose again between them, pierced only by the periodic pops and snaps of the dry wood blazing in the fireplace.

Accustomed to the noise of blaring stereos, thunderous footsteps from the second floor, and a continually ringing telephone, April found this tomblike atmosphere torturous. Each time the wood crackled, she flinched.

Some harmony house. They had no television, no radio, no newspapers or books, nothing to counter the endless monotony except a bookshelf full of board games and each other. So April had a choice: talk to Jeff or play Parcheesi.

She cleared her throat with a loud "ahem" and asked, "Wanna play Parcheesi?"

Chicken.

"No, thanks," he replied from his seat near the fire.

"Monopoly? Scrabble? Trivial Pursuit?" She continued reading the names from the boxes on the shelf before her, but hope that he'd agree to something slowly faded.

"No, no, no."

"Read any good books lately?"

He looked up from the fireplace and offered her a bland smile. "Unfortunately, no."

Oh, for God's sake! At last, she retorted, "Well, what do *you* wanna do?"

One perfect eyebrow arched in her direction. "Why are you so jumpy? Sit. Enjoy the quiet for a while."

Enjoy the quiet? Fat chance. Quiet left her brain unoccupied, gave her time to think. Thinking was bad. Thinking led to second-guessing. Like wondering why she'd signed up for this torture to begin with. No, quiet was definitely not something she enjoyed. She never should have agreed to stay here, never should have appeared on the talk show, never should have—

Anxiety propelled her to her feet. "You know what? I think I'm ready to say good night."

"Okay." His attention returned to the fireplace. "I'll give you some privacy and join you there in a little while."

While her brain continued its traipse over all the mistakes she'd made in her life, her trembling legs managed to carry her to the bedroom.

Nerves caused goose bumps to rise on her skin as she stared at the pile of nightshirts and chemises tucked into the dresser drawer. Since her divorce, she'd always had her bedroom to herself and normally slept in something light, pretty, and lacy. But with Jeff's presence and nothing but a simple sheet separating them— a sheet that could become transparent with the wrong backdrop of light—throwing on a teensy-weensy nightie became as likely as the possibility of her sprouting wings and flying from Harmony House.

Now what would she do?

When no other option blossomed in her infertile brain, April settled on a pair of sweats and a T-shirt. With the garments tucked in her arms, she fled to the bathroom, where she quickly changed, washed her face, and brushed her teeth.

By the time she slipped into the bedroom, Jeff's shadow moved across the other side of the sheet. Before he might notice her, she dove under the covers, like a stealth bomber headed to the hangar. Ridiculous, really, but her imagination pictured Jeff ogling her silhouette like some badly drawn cartoon wolf. Her stomach flipped, and she placed a palm flat against her abdomen until the flutters eased.

Tucked in for the night, she peered at the sheet suspended between them. What did he sleep in? *Hmmph!* From what she'd seen of him so far, she'd guess a guy with his air of self-confidence probably slept in nothing but a smile.

Not that she intended to peek.

Minutes ticked by with the speed of a comatose slug. That wall of silence built up between them again, more solid than the sheet, yet invisible to the naked eye. It covered her like a wet blanket, suffocating her. Either the good doctor was a sound sleeper, or he was doing his best to feign slumber to avoid talking to her.

Fine. She punched the pillow and lay flat, staring up. She didn't want to talk to him either.

Moonbeams filtered in through the skylight above her bed, leaving a dappled shade on her covered legs. For lack of anything better to do, she held her hands out to play with the glow and shadows. If she extended two fingers upward, she could make a bunny. One finger extended downward created an elephant.

Thumper, she told her left hand, *meet Dumbo.*

A derisive snort escaped her lips.

Perfect! Day One and I'm already making Disney shadow puppets on the bedcovers. By the time we reach Day Thirty, I'll probably be a babbling idiot.

God, how she hated being here. She missed her kids, her home, her bed, her television. She missed Bette Davis.

April had first become addicted to old movies during Becky's midnight feedings. The late shows were the only things on network TV in the wee hours. And even after both kids began sleeping through the night, April still snuggled on the couch with the black-and-white images of Joan Crawford, Bette Davis, and Katharine Hepburn for company. Now she realized how much she missed their companionship.

The goddesses of fifties cinema always seemed to have the right look, the right man, the right answer.

But April didn't. April never did.

On the other side of the room, the visions Jeff forced out of his mind during the day assailed him. Always the same visions . . .

A triumphant Emma in a beaded oyster-colored sheath, accepting her first Daytime Television Award. Emma as the blushing bride, a whisper-transparent veil enhancing her beauty rather than hiding it. The raw emotions of fear and joy etched on her face the day she told him she was pregnant. Emma lying in a satin-lined coffin, beauty frozen in time, like Snow White.

And finally, the stern visage of the obstetrician who asked, "Didn't you know your wife had a problem?"

No.

This admission became his greatest shame. Jefferson Prentiss, PhD, had earned a reputation as a caring, intuitive psychologist. Yet he'd never known the depths of his own wife's dangerous habits.

Yes, she'd been a terrific actress, but why hadn't he seen the changes in her? A first-year med student could have picked up on the laundry list of symptoms. The restlessness, the insomnia, the loss of appetite, the mood swings—she blamed it all on the pregnancy. And he, blissful in his ignorance, turned a blind eye to his wife and the secret slowly destroying her.

Wrapped up in making a success of his practice, he'd forgotten all about Emma the person. He saw her only as the wife waiting for him when he finally got home at night, someone who placed dinner before him, listened to his complaints about his workday, and lay beside him in their bed. He relegated her to second-class status in their marriage and, in doing so, destroyed the love she'd sworn would last until death did them part.

She never blamed him, never accused him of abandoning her.

She merely occupied her time with methods meant to improve her appearance and recapture his waning attention—methods that had eventually killed her and their child.

Their son, Michael Alexander Prentiss, had lived for two minutes outside his mother's body. One hundred and twenty brief seconds. Not even long enough to dream. There would be no firsts for Michael: no first word, first step, or first birthday. Not even a first *day.*

Every night, the image of Michael's dying body—a tiny purple-hued boy in a plastic case, struggling to hold on to life for one more minute, and failing miserably—floated above Jeff's conscience.

I let him down. I let them both down.

Chapter Nine

T he rich, nutty smell of coffee tickled April's nostrils, rousing her in a way a buzzing alarm clock never had—subtly, sensually, one heavenly sniff at a time. She couldn't decide whether to get up and follow the hypnotic odor or snuggle deeper into the blankets for more sleep. Her eyelids fluttered once, twice, but she didn't have the energy to fully open them, no matter how intoxicating the scent around her was.

The coffee's aroma mingled with spicy cologne: cloves, one of her favorite smells. Content to allow her other senses to revel in the stimulants they experienced, she refused to open her eyes.

"Wake up, darling," a male voice whispered low in her ear.

"Mmmm," she sighed, and rolled over. "Five more minutes . . ."

Hold it. A male voice? In her bedroom? And calling her darling?

She sat bolt upright in the bed, her eyes round and wide, her heart pounding. Her hands clawed at the blankets until she clutched them to her chin. When her vision finally focused, Jeff's solid frame and easy smile registered on her frantic brain cells.

She let out a deep sigh of relief. "You scared me to death!"

"Sorry."

Jeff was already dressed in a sweater-and-jeans ensemble. The sweater had a charcoal-gray shadow-stripe pattern. The hue brought silver glints to his eyes, like dew sparkling on freshly mowed grass.

Wake up, sweetie! It's a little too early in the morning to wax poetic.

"I brought you a cup of coffee," he said, indicating the white mug he held. "David will be here in an hour. You'll probably want to shower and dress before he arrives, and it's important we discuss how we're going to handle today's interview. Privately."

Only one sentence in his little speech registered in her sleep-filled mind. "You . . . brought me . . . coffee?"

God, she sounded like the heroine in a bad comic-book movie—ready to swoon because the hero brought her the magic elixir of life. But no one had ever brought her coffee in bed before—not even on Mother's Day or her birthday.

Squelching ripples of delight, she reached to take the mug from him. It really was coffee, and it was still hot. She sipped the brew, and the spicy tang tickled her tongue.

"Thanks, Jeff. This was just what I needed before today's torture begins."

"No charge," he said as he took the cup from her and headed toward the door. "There's a full pot downstairs when you're ready. For now, I'll give you some time to get up, shower, and dress. But don't take too long. We want to rehearse what we're going to say to Grant and Jocelyn before David shows up and starts screeching about spontaneity."

Once she was certain he'd returned to the kitchen, she tossed off the blankets and rose from her bed. Stretching the kinks out of her back, she heaved a deep sigh. The last two people she wanted to face today were Satan's sidekicks—Grant and Jocelyn. At least having Jeff on her side, rather than against her, would ease today's interview. The man exuded confidence—not to mention sex appeal.

She shook her head to dislodge her bizarre thoughts.

April, honey, you really have to get ahold of yourself. Remember that song from South Pacific.

With a broad smile stretching across her cheeks, she broke into a chorus of "I'm Gonna Wash That Man Right Outa My Hair."

Yes, indeed. A nice hot shower is what I need to clear the idiocy from my brains.

She strolled into the bathroom humming her new mantra and stopped short before the sink. *Ah, and so it begins,* she thought with disgust. Globs of green shaving gel and black stubble coated the basin. He couldn't have taken a minute to rinse this filth out? So much for being thankful Jeff was with her.

Her sharp gaze caught the camera perched above the medicine cabinet. "Are you getting all this?" she asked the fish-eye lens. "Day One and I'm already cleaning up after him."

She wiped the offensive mess from the pink porcelain with a sheaf of toilet paper. Come to think of it, she'd probably have no trouble at all considering Jeff the enemy. Provided he'd continue to act like the typical male she so often cleaned up after, she'd win this challenge hands down.

April and Jeff sat on the plaid couch in Harmony House's living room. Twin black wires, attached to earphones they wore to hear the hosts of *Taking Sides,* dangled from their necks. Near the dining room, a dozen men, including David, stood behind two large mounted television cameras, transferring their live feed to the studio audience in Manhattan.

April's nerves caused her to teeter on the edge of madness as she sat, false smile plastered to her face. *Let the insanity begin.*

"Well, Jeff, April, why don't you tell us about your first evening together?" Jocelyn's voice sang in April's ear.

"It went quite well, Jocelyn," Jeff replied, calm and easy. "We began building a rapport immediately upon our arrival."

"Did you encounter any problems with our plans for you?" Grant asked.

The pointed manner in which he'd asked the question made the show's aim perfectly clear. They intended to jump right into the single-bedroom issue. Jeff had been absolutely correct. David had planned that little surprise so the audience could see their reactions first thing in the morning.

Well, she and Jeff were ready. They'd rehearsed their responses while making the beds in the one room they knew had no cameras. Now Jeff glanced in April's direction and gave a barely perceptible nod. It was time to recite her lines.

"Nothing too catastrophic," she assured them with a warm smile. "Jeff and I disagreed with some of the arrangements that were made prior to our arrival—"

"Such as?" Jocelyn persisted.

Yup. This was exactly how they'd figured the interview would play out. April was prepared for their pit bull mentality, thanks to Jeff's coaching. *Tell the audience the truth,* he had advised, *and let them make up their own minds.*

"April?" Jocelyn prompted. "What sort of things did you and Jeff have issues with?"

Here goes nothing.

"Our sleeping arrangements, for one thing."

"Oh, that's right. You're sharing a bedroom, aren't you?"

The shocked gasps from the audience whistled through her earpiece, and she jumped in reaction. Jeff took hold of her hand, exerting a little pressure and a silent communication of what was already running through her head: *Steady, April. Say your lines the way we rehearsed them.*

"How exactly did you settle that problem?" Jocelyn asked.

"Really, Jocelyn." She forced a lighthearted giggle. "Dr. Jeff and I are adults. There are some aspects of our time here that we insist upon keeping private."

Dead air surrounded them for a full minute. *Victory!* Her response apparently had flustered Jocelyn into silence—no small feat.

"So," Grant said, finally breaking the quiet. "It would seem that your theories are working, Dr. Jeff. Wouldn't you agree?"

"I think it's much too early to say that, Grant," Jeff replied. "After all, April and I have been together less than twenty-four hours."

"Then what would you call the rapport so obviously blossoming between you two?"

"The calm before the storm?" April suggested.

Jeff burst out laughing. Unfortunately, as far as April could tell, no one else did. She would have cringed, but the camera's red eye stared in her face, serving as a reminder that a nationwide audience viewed her every action.

"Are you that unhappy with your situation, then, April?" Grant asked.

Oh, God. Had she frowned on camera? It was time for some serious damage control. "Of course not," she replied. "I was joking about the storm."

"The truth is," Jeff said, "from the moment we arrived here, April and I discovered we have an amazing synchronicity."

"We have some video of your 'amazing synchronicity' last night." Jocelyn had found her voice again. What a pity. "What do you say, ladies and gentlemen? Would you like to see how well Dr. Jeff and April *really* handled their little surprise yesterday?"

The audience's roar of approval nearly deafened her. At that moment, if April had had a shovel nearby, she'd have dug a hole to China. Judging by Jeff's grimace, she knew he'd have been right beside her, digging at the same furious pace. Rather than agreeing to spend a month in Harmony House, they should have held out for twin root canals without anesthetic. At least that kind of pain ended quickly.

But this? This was pure torture. She frantically reviewed in her mind everything she and Jeff had done and said yesterday, hoping for a clue to what they were about to hear.

She had to hand it to the show's hosts. They sure knew how to drag out the tension. Sweat, due somewhat to the lights, but more to anticipation, beaded her forehead.

In their cozy living room, on their stiff-backed couch, she and Jeff were at a distinct disadvantage. They didn't have a video screen or a closed-circuit television. They had nothing to discern what was happening in the studio but their acute sense of hearing.

The crackle of static assailed her eardrums, and then: "What do you mean there's only one bedroom?"

Good God, was that *her* voice, sounding so terrified? What was the audience doing now? Were they laughing at her? Did they feel her fear? Did they pity her? Did they hate her?

She didn't have time to ponder, because Jeff's voice thundered inside her head. "You knew we wouldn't be happy with the sleeping arrangements. So what's the deal? Was this supposed to be our first episode? Filming our outraged reactions?"

Oooh! April shivered. This was outright devious. Someone on the production team had sliced and spliced their disagreement with David to look like tag-team temper tantrums.

"You actually told our executive producer, David Darwin, that you would leave Harmony House," Jocelyn said. "Didn't you, April?"

April's mouth went dry, and words flew from her brain, leaving nothing but gibberish.

Quick. What would Bette Davis say?

For the first time ever, her favorite movie heroine deserted her.

To heck with Bette Davis. What should April Raine say?

The silence lengthened. A roar filled her ears. She needed an answer fast. Suddenly, Jeff's advice whispered inside her head. *Tell the truth, and let the audience make up their own minds.*

"Yes, Jocelyn, that's true," she said, "but that was before Dr. Jeff and I came up with our reasonable compromise."

"And what was that compromise?" Jocelyn asked archly.

Clever woman. But not clever enough.

April shared a quick smile with Jeff, who nodded slightly, communicating reassurance louder than a team of cheerleaders.

"I've already told you. There are some subjects that Dr. Jeff and I will not discuss."

Bette Davis would be proud. . . .

"Well, I'm sure we'll be learning more about each of you over the next four weeks." Jocelyn giggled. "Goodness, by the time this month is up, I wonder if either of you will have any secrets left!"

Fear slammed into April like an iceberg hitting the *Titanic*. Would they really learn her secrets? She had only one secret she refused to share: the secret about her son.

Not that she was ashamed of Michael. His handicap wasn't his fault, wasn't anyone's fault. But that didn't mean she wanted either of her children put under the talk show microscope for publicity, especially Michael, who could never understand.

Jeff crossed one leg over the other, jostling April out of her reverie. "You're assuming we have secrets to begin with."

"*Everyone* has secrets, Dr. Jeff," Jocelyn replied.

Was April imagining the sudden tightness to his posture? She stole a quick glance in his direction, but his bland expression communicated nothing.

"Thanks so much for talking with us today, Dr. Jeff, April," Grant said. "Enjoy the rest of your day, and we look forward to seeing you again tomorrow. Ladies and gents, stay tuned. Coming up next, we'll hear a song from the new superstar hitting the top of the country music charts . . ."

April's lower jaw clunked against her chest. That was it? No mention of how she'd had to clean his gunk out of the sink this morning? Not even some mindless chatter about Jeff making her coffee and serving it in bed? After all, with his sweet gesture and her bathroom cleanup, they had each scored a point for their side of the argument this morning. Yet Grant and Jocelyn preferred to showcase that stupid problem with the bedroom.

Was this what she could expect every day? Simple scenes that showed the worst of them with nothing encouraging or even remotely related to the debate that brought them here? Brainless titillation and innuendo? The sneaky suspicion that this entire setup had been planned to humiliate her reared its ugly head again. This time, though, it refused to be banished.

What else would they do to her over the next thirty days? Did they plan to choose a winner by holding a swimsuit competition? How low would she be forced to sink in this farce? And how much business would she wind up losing because of her participation here?

She never should have signed on to this stupidity.

Not even twenty-four hours in and I'm already regretting my decision. Surely, this does not bode well.

Summer Raine Jackson clicked off the television and stared at the remote control with envy. Lucky April. Like a cat thrown from a second story, April always landed on her feet. Now she had the opportunity to spend a whole month living with that scrumptious Dr. Jeff.

Until now, Summer had never envied her big sister, who had gotten pregnant at seventeen, dropped out of high school, and married a loser who cheated on her every chance he got.

No, Summer had never felt the slightest twinge of envy. She'd never had a reason to—until now.

Because now a crack had appeared in her flawless world. And if she pressed against it too hard, her entire life would shatter.

Stop. Don't think about where Brad might have been last night. Think about the good things. You have a beautiful home, a wonderful life. . . .

But what if the life she valued was over?

She forced herself to her feet. Nothing was over. She had to stop letting her imagination get the better of her. Just because April's husband had cheated didn't mean her husband was fated to follow suit. There had to be a logical explanation for why she hadn't been able to reach Brad at the office last night. Maybe he had turned off his phone so he wouldn't be interrupted by a call from an insecure wife.

Yes, she told herself, fluffing the throw pillows with forceful fists. That was it. *See? A simple explanation. No reason to jump to crazy conclusions. Absolutely none.*

Why, when he came home after work today, she wouldn't even mention last night's unanswered phone call. She wasn't some jealous harpy ready to pounce on her husband for forgetting to check in with her. Brad was a loving, loyal man who'd never given her any reason to suspect him of infidelity.

Six hours later, when Brad finally opened the front door, candlelight danced in silver tapers on the glossy cherry dining room table. The aroma of tilapia in citrus, his favorite meal, filled the house. Summer approached him, a seductive smile on her face, and a filled martini glass in her hand.

He inhaled deeply, took the glass, and sipped. Instantly, the tense lines on his forehead eased, and he sighed. Mission accomplished.

"Wow," he said, his eyes wide with surprise. "This is great, Sum. What's the occasion?"

"Where were you last night, Brad?" The words exploded before she could attempt to stop them.

"Last night?" He took a sip of the martini, then swallowed. "I was at work. I told you, I had a conference call with Hong Kong and then some paperwork to clean up afterward."

Summer's stomach kinked into knots of fear. "I called your office. Around eleven. You didn't pick up."

"Was that you?" Leaning forward, he kissed her cheek. "I'm sorry, babe. I thought it was Botsoi calling back to renegotiate the fees I'd just wrangled out of him. After all the hours I put in on his contract, I wasn't about to give him the opportunity to weasel out of the deal." He flashed her that lopsided grin that always weakened her knees. "Had I known it was you, I definitely would have picked up."

Relief flooded Summer's skeleton, easing the tightness she'd slept with instead of her husband. She believed him. Why wouldn't she? She trusted him.

What choice did she have?

Chapter Ten

Once the interview came to an end, David and the cameramen left as quickly as they'd arrived. Jeff faced an entire day filled with nothing to do—with April.

Well, he should use the opportunity to get to know her, find her weak spots—if she had any. . . .

Together, they made an early lunch and sat in the dining room, separated by a long expanse of gleaming cherry wood.

"Did the show go the way you thought it would?" April asked.

"I expected them to lead with the one-bedroom issue," he replied, "but I also figured they'd air other moments. It was a little disconcerting, wasn't it?"

"Not compared to undergoing a C-section with a grapefruit spoon." She held up the offensive article, and the ceiling fan's light glinted off its sawlike edge.

He laughed. "You have much experience with kitchen utensil deliveries?"

"Well, I did contemplate it when I was in labor with my son. Fourteen hours is an awfully long time to deal with a baby who insists upon swinging from your intestines before leaving the womb."

"I would imagine so. Tell me about your children."

At the mere mention of her family, her face took on a golden glow, and her eyes sparkled with love and pride. "I have two. My daughter, Becky, is eighteen."

"And as gorgeous as her mother, I bet."

Her cheeks bloomed the hue of the ruby red grapefruit on her plate. "She resembles me, yes. But she adds different colors to her hair to reduce the comparisons from strangers. Let's face it. Most kids do *not* want to be told they look just like their mom. For some strange reason, they don't see it as a compliment. So one week, Becky will have red streaks in her hair. Another week, she'll sport bright purple stripes. I bet if she could figure out a way to go plaid, she'd make her hair resemble a Scotsman's kilt." With a giggle, she shook her head. "Teenagers. They have a unique style adults can't begin to fathom."

"I think it's wise of you to let her make her own choices on personal decisions. It gives her some modicum of power. Many parents might not be as lenient."

"Oh, well, I'm a firm believer in not sweating the small stuff. I sometimes think if my mother hadn't been so strict with me . . ."

Her voice trailed off in obvious embarrassment, and the blush in her cheeks became a red flush that traveled down her neck. She must have remembered that the mounted cameras were recording everything she said.

"You're absolutely right, April." He hastened to reassure her. "The tighter the reins we keep on our children, the more they rebel against our authority."

She sighed and picked at her grapefruit with the spoon. "I hope so. She's smarter than I was at her age. At least, I think she's smarter. Unfortunately, I won't know the truth until she's all grown up and happy in her life. My biggest fear is that she'll wind up making the same mistakes I did."

"What kind of mistakes?"

"Marrying young. Relying on someone else rather than herself. Independence is the greatest gift we're given in life. Unfortunately, I had to learn that lesson the hard way." Apparently finished toying with her food, she set the spoon aside and stared at him. "You know, you're very easy to talk to."

He shrugged. "I'm a psychologist. It comes with the territory."

"Your wife must have appreciated that about you."

Probably. If she'd ever known it. But, of course, she'd taken solace elsewhere. He shook his head to clear the visions once again invading his brain. "You have a son also?"

"Mmm-hmm. Michael is twelve."

Michael. Regret pierced his chest. His Michael would have been looking forward to his sixth birthday soon. With tremendous effort, he took a deep breath. Disregarding the pain the effort cost, he pasted a bland smile on his face. "And does he look like you?"

"No, not really."

Relief eased his heartache when she didn't elaborate.

Instead, she cast another glance toward the camera mounted above the pantry. "You know what? I think I need to take a walk. I get stir-crazy sitting in the house all day."

He rose from his chair, leaving the rest of his lunch untouched. "I'll go with you." Not because he wanted to, but because the idea of staying alone in this room with his thoughts constricted his chest.

"Great," she said, but her tone suggested that great was far from what she really thought of the idea.

Cool air expanded her lungs, ridding her of the claustrophobia she'd experienced in the dining room. She blamed the cameras. Knowing that a national audience watched every move she made inhibited her to the point of stupidity. She found herself rethinking each action and choice before committing to it.

And no doubt her hesitation would leave the viewers at home thinking *Taking Sides* had saddled Dr. Jeff with a blithering idiot at Harmony House.

"The cameras are getting to you, right?" Jeff's voice intruded into her thoughts like nails on a chalkboard.

She turned away from him and scanned the line of pine trees sticking up out of the mountains. She hoped he'd read the hint and give her a little breathing room.

"Or maybe I'm to blame," he said, and walked to the opposite side of the rocky ledge.

Ouch.

Okay, so he'd read her loud and clear. Maybe a little too loud and too clear. The flames of embarrassment crept up from her throat to her ears. Here she was, acting like a first-class witch. And for what?

Jeff had gone out of his way to be nice to her. He'd brought her coffee in bed, for goodness sake.

She sighed.

Obviously, she owed him another apology. At this rate she'd probably make *The Guinness Book of World Records* before the month ended. But under what heading? Stupidest Woman Alive? Or Most Mea Culpas in a Thirty-Day Period?

Unfortunately, she wasn't very good at apologizing. She'd never had much practice. During her marriage, she'd been the *apologizee,* not the apologizer . . . or . . . apologist. Whatever.

It was time to refer to the pros for some assistance. What would Bette Davis do in this situation? *Ha. Easy.* She'd blame Joan Crawford. Joan would insist Jeff apologize to *her,* and Katharine Hepburn could wangle that apology from Jeff with a simple smile. Well, if her favorite movie heroines didn't plan to help, April would have to come up with some sort of atonement on her own.

On a deep inhale for fortitude, she turned and walked toward the bluff where Jeff stood. "You know what?" she said with forced cheerfulness.

He looked at her over his shoulder, his mouth etched in a deep scowl. "What?"

"I just had a great idea. It's such a nice day today. How about if we pack up the rest of the unfinished lunch sitting in the dining room and have a picnic right here, overlooking the stream?"

The scowl relaxed, but one eyebrow rose in disbelief. "It's forty degrees outside."

"We can wear our jackets. And I'll brew a fresh pot of coffee. What do you say?"

While he hesitated in making up his mind, she hopped from one foot to the other, like a kid about to wet her pants, waiting for his reply.

At last he said, "All right. It sounds nice, actually."

Her breath came out in one long whoosh. Odd, she'd forgotten to inhale or exhale since making him the offer. She stubbornly refused to examine why.

"Good," she said, then flashed a challenging grin in his direction. "I'll race you home."

With a sudden burst of speed, she took off down the slight incline toward the walkway and the house. Something about the freedom of the outdoors had flipped a switch inside her head. Adrenaline coursed through her veins, providing a rush of joyful energy she hadn't experienced since receiving her divorce papers in the mail.

What a great day that had turned into. Her neighbors must have thought she needed psychological help when they saw her doing cartwheels on the lawn, but she didn't care. And of course, now she had a psychologist on her heels.

How far back was he, anyway? She craned her neck to look over her shoulder and then screeched. Jeff ran close behind, gaining fast.

On a new burst of speed, she hit the curved path of white pebbles near the front door. But he caught up too quickly. Before she could blink, he passed by her in a blur of color. In four long-legged strides, he scaled the steps and stopped on the porch, a huge male-chauvinist smile plastered on his face.

"I should have warned you," he said between huffs and puffs. "I lettered in track at Harvard."

Despite her own breathlessness, she offered him a mock frown. "Serves me right for challenging you without knowing your scholastic history."

They entered the house, and April's gaze connected with the camera staring at them. She smiled.

What would the viewers at home think about this? She and Jeff had walked out of here a short while ago, a heavy resentment building between them, and now returned panting and sweaty.

The thought of the insidious theories spinning around office cubicles and book club meetings tomorrow nearly sent her into a fit of giggles. She managed to swallow them back with one loud, unladylike snort.

"Stop that." He chastised her from the foyer.

She steamed up with embarrassment.

Still, she decided to feign ignorance. "Stop what?"

"I know what you're thinking." As if to confirm it, he casually nodded at the camera dangling from the loft's railing. "And it isn't funny."

Inside her head, an invisible imp egged her on. "Not even a little?"

His lips quirked, but he managed to fight back his own laughter. "No, not at all."

"Bummer. It sure seems funny."

He folded his arms over his chest and gave her what she suspected was his best laughing-on-the-inside-but-not-showing-it-on-the-outside glare. "I thought you were going to make coffee."

"Okay, okay," she said, relenting. "While I'm doing that, why don't you grab the king-sized blanket to spread on the grass?"

Let the audience think what they wanted about *that* request. She hadn't the slightest intention of enlightening them.

Chapter Eleven

Tell me about your family," Jeff said.

They sat together on the grassy ledge, eating the Waldorf chicken salad they'd made for lunch.

April paused, a forkful of chicken and raisins midway between her chin and open mouth. "I thought I already did."

"You told me about your children. What about the rest of your family? Are your parents still alive?"

"My mother is." As usual when the topic of her mother arose, her lips tightened into a grim line. Catching herself, she relaxed her facial muscles again. "My father passed away eight years ago. Heart attack."

"I'm sorry."

She shrugged. "The worst part is that he never got to see me make a success out of life." Flames licked her cheeks. God, he probably thought she considered herself some international hotshot now. "What I mean is—"

Jeff held up a hand. "Relax, April. I understand what you're saying. He never knew about your business and what you've achieved."

She took a deep, cleansing breath and exhaled. "Yeah. Something like that."

"Regardless of how old we grow, we all crave our parents' approval. Losing your father before you could fulfill that basic need must be tough for you."

A lump rose in her throat, and she swallowed hard. "What about your parents?"

He grinned. "Uh-uh. It's your turn in this spotlight without a spotlight." His hands encompassed the forest around them. "No cameras, no excuses. Later, you can question me."

"Chicken," she grumbled.

He winked, sending a frisson of delight through her veins. "Do you have any siblings?"

Delight evaporated. "Two. Both younger. One of them, Summer, lives near me."

"That must be nice."

The tight-lipped smile returned. This time, she required a lot more effort to relax her facial muscles. "You think so?"

"It isn't?"

"It's like having two mothers within walking distance of every tragic mistake you've ever made."

"Why is that?"

She stabbed at the chicken chunks on her plate, shredding them with the fork's tines. "Because Summer is everything I'm not, and she uses most of any time we spend together instructing me on what's wrong with my life."

"Could that be sibling rivalry speaking?"

She considered the idea, playing with it in her brain the way she'd tongue a sore tooth. Jeff wasn't the first person to suggest that her animosity toward Summer might be jealousy. As a matter of fact, Peter used to accuse her of envying both her sisters on a regular basis.

"Maybe it *is* sibling rivalry," she conceded. "But for as long as I can remember, Mom has always compared me to Summer, and I've never measured up."

"Give me an example, if you can."

Ha! Easy. Hundreds of Mom's disparaging remarks lay cataloged in her memory, like a scrapbook she could take out and peruse whenever the doldrums ruled her mind. But for Jeff, who'd probably heard some real horror stories in his profession, she needed more than the run-of-the-mill why-can't-you-be-more-like-your-sister illustration. She needed the Whopper, the *Titanic* of Mom's criticisms. And she knew exactly which page to flip to.

"Okay. When Peter and I were first dating, I brought him home to meet my family. I thought it went well, but afterwards, while we were washing the dishes, I pulled Mom aside to get her honest opinion of him. She told me that someone as good-looking as Peter couldn't possibly be interested in a girl like me. She claimed he must have been dating me to get to Summer. 'After all,' she told me, 'Summer is so much prettier than you.' "

Years later, on a grassy ledge, as she dined beside another good-looking man, her mother's words still stung. While her heart splintered at the memory, April stared across the gray-flannel sky and blinked away tears.

When she spoke again, pain scraped her throat raw. "Can you imagine a mother would actually say something like that to her own daughter? Of course, if I were to remind my mother now of what she'd said that evening, she'd tell me I'm too sensitive or I'm overreacting or she said it for my own good."

Embarrassment sent new heat hurtling to her cheeks, and she shivered as the memories dissipated. Jeff stared at her, his face impassive, but his eyes narrowed with interest.

Darn it. She'd rambled—about an incident that had happened twenty years earlier.

He probably thinks I'm a complete basket case now.

Feigning indifference, she lifted her Styrofoam cup and sipped.

"Why do you think your mother considers Summer so wonderful?"

April nearly choked on her coffee. "Are you kidding? She's *every* mother's dream. You know the type. You probably treat them in therapy sessions for obsessive-compulsive disorder. Summer was the daughter who never got dirty as a kid. No skinned knees or stained jeans for Summer. Straight-A student, queen of the prom in both junior and senior year, got a degree from a local college, landed a job in a department store and worked her way up the retail chain to become a marketing and research bigshot, then married a man just like dear old Dad and settled down to keep a beautiful home." The sarcasm rose high inside her. And she let her bitterness spew. "Summer's the perfect little hausfrau. You'd love her."

"I see," he said, nodding. "Unlike you, who . . ."

"Got pregnant and married a 'bum' before I finished high

school," she finished for him while counting her sins on her fingers. "If that wasn't scandalous enough, I divorced the bum at twenty-nine, and nearly seven years later, I still haven't found an ideal man to make Mom proud. Regardless of any success with my company, without a man in my life, I'm floundering as far as she's concerned."

His gaze remained steady on her face, his expression unreadable. "Why? Because you're not as perfect as Summer?"

Oh, she wasn't even close in that competition. But she bit back the comment before it escaped. Another sip of coffee to buy time and regain her placid veneer, and then she remarked, "Honestly? I sometimes wonder about Summer. I mean, nobody's life is *that* perfect." She gazed across the line of pine and birch trees to the rocky glen in the distance. Lemon sunlight glinted off the wall of boulders in crazy diamonds. "You know what I think?"

"What?"

"I think one day, the pressure's going to be too much and she's gonna snap. Maybe go berserk in a Pier 1 or something."

Jeff chuckled, and her blood tingled with that familiar thrill. How liberating to find a guy who understood her sense of humor!

"What about your other sister? Does she feel the same way about Summer?"

Ah, yes. Her other sister. April fought a grimace and pointed to the Thermos. If she had to discuss her family life in so much detail, she'd need more coffee.

Jeff lifted the canister and refilled her cup.

She held the cup to her nose, allowed the caffeine to enter her body through her nasal passages. When that didn't bolster enough confidence, she took a slow, steady drink. Finally, she could put off the inevitable no longer.

"Brooklyn never competed with Summer. She didn't have to. She was Dad's favorite. No one rivaled the great Brooklyn Raine."

"Wait a minute." He froze, Thermos poised over his cup, and stared, eyes wide. "Brooklyn Raine is your sister? As in world-class ski champion—"

"And Olympic gold medalist in the giant slalom," she reminded him. Why try to hide her resentment? He'd probably pick up on her mixed emotions anyway. "Don't forget that."

He set the Thermos on the blanket and replaced the cap. "Wow. I'm impressed."

She gulped the rest of her coffee, ignoring the searing heat in her throat. "So is everyone else."

"No. I don't mean it that way. I mean, it must have been tough growing up with that kind of celebrity in your family."

The breeze rustled through her, and she shivered. "I didn't exactly grow up with it. Once she started making a name in the sports world, she and Dad were on the circuit nine months out of the year."

"Yeah, but still. For a while, a person couldn't buy a breakfast cereal or a lip balm without seeing Brooklyn Raine's face plastered on the package. And you would have to face that kind of celebrity every day. Every morning before school, every afternoon while watching television. How did you handle it? Did you get harassed by people wanting autographs or special favors?"

She shrugged. "No one knew, really. I mean, of course some people knew. But my father was a barracuda about keeping Brooklyn away from the media as much as possible while she competed. That meant no interviews, no photo ops, no links between her family at home and her professional career on the slopes. I mean, could you imagine if someone in the press had discovered that while snow-white Brooklyn wowed the crowds in Canada, her older sister was telling Mom about an upcoming surprise baby?" She rounded her eyes and covered her open mouth with a hand. "Horrors!"

Shaking his head, Jeff clucked his tongue. "Shocking indeed. Such an event could bring about the fall of democracy as we know it."

"Yeah, well, in my parents' household, my pregnancy was pretty darn close to the first sign of the apocalypse." She grimaced. "The stigma could not be allowed to taint the family's sterling reputation. So I was persona non grata until Brooklyn officially retired from the pro circuit."

"And then she just seemed to fade away." His long fingers danced over the air as if releasing dust into the breeze.

"Like Garbo," April said on a heavy sigh.

"Where is she these days?"

"Garbo? She died. In 1990, I think."

His humor erupted in an exhale of breath. "Nice try, April, but I meant your sister."

"Brooklyn?"

She feigned indifference, but her senses went on red alert. To this day, Brooklyn despised the press and insisted on total hermit status. Only her immediate family knew her whereabouts. Outsiders were kept to the information available in old newspapers and magazines.

What should she do? Since she wasn't certain how much she could trust him, she fell back on the standard line. "Brooklyn lives in a remote ski town in the mountains. Married Canadian ski champ Marc Cheviot and planned an idyllic life with lots of kids who'd inherit their stellar talents."

With a pleased smile, Jeff nodded. "Good for them."

"Mmmm. Not so good. Six months after they married, Marc was diagnosed with pancreatic cancer."

"Sheesh!" Jeff whistled through his teeth.

"He died on their fourth wedding anniversary."

"That's a heartbreaker."

She toyed with her empty cup and thought about her sister: how miserable Lyn had looked the last time she'd seen her, how she seemed simply to stagnate, never breaking out of the safe little box she'd created in Snowed Inn Bed and Breakfast.

"She doesn't talk about her ski days. I guess losing the two men who appreciated the sport as much as she did—her husband and her dad—in the same year affected her more deeply than we thought."

"What makes you say that?"

April sighed. "Do you have any idea how many sports shows and magazines still clamor for an interview with her? But, just like Garbo, she shut herself off from the rest of the world."

"That's not healthy," Jeff remarked with a frown.

"Well, I'm exaggerating a little. She runs her b-and-b, does some charity work, and still skis every chance she gets. Just not in competitions. Nor does she want to go back to celebrity status. I think she did all those promotions and commercials because my dad wanted her to." The bitterness crawled up her esophagus like acid. "And Daddy's little darling always did what Daddy wanted."

"So you have one sister who is Mama's darling, and one sister who was Daddy's darling."

He covered her icy hand with his much warmer one and leaned close. His eyes bored into hers, conveying sympathy, understanding, and something more—something akin to affection.

Overwhelming heat suffused her face. Despite the chill in the air, perspiration beaded her flesh. Beneath her rib cage, her heartbeat accelerated to the pace of a hummingbird's. If he decided to kiss her at this moment, she'd give in. Wholly.

"Whose darling are you, April Raine?"

The question took her by surprise. But the answer shattered the illusions of heat, kissing, and two people, hands entwined, on a blanket atop a mountain ledge. The chicken salad threatened to revolt in her throat, and she swallowed it along with a tremendous dose of self-pity.

"Nobody's," she admitted in a choked voice. "Absolutely nobody's."

Chapter Twelve

Jeff followed April into the house and closed the door, resisting the urge to lean against the jamb and watch her every move. When she headed for the kitchen and turned on the faucet, he hung back.

She needed some time without his hovering presence. That was nearly impossible in their current circumstances, but he'd try his best to allow her a little solitude.

While she washed the lunch dishes, he fussed with kindling and paper in the fireplace.

Sympathy and guilt mingled in the air around him like soot from the chimney. Who knew that April had such an interesting, soft underbelly? He'd never intended to probe her family relationships so deeply. It had started out as idle conversation. Somewhere along the way, the psychologist in him took over.

You can take the analyst out of the office . . .

April's inferiority complex and the unresolved issues with her mother and sisters piqued his curiosity. He was amazed that with a family dynamic like hers, April hadn't wound up hooked on drugs or alcohol. She wouldn't be the first person to attempt to compensate for feelings of inadequacy with a headlong dive into substance abuse. Bitter experience had taught him that much.

Had he done the right thing by dropping the subject after her piteous confession that she was nobody's darling? As a professional, he would have loved to continue their discussion. But she wasn't his patient.

Besides, he'd already pushed her too far. Pools of unshed tears had glistened in her eyes while they'd packed up the picnic leftovers. She practically ran down the hill to get back here. It wasn't a fun-loving sprint like she'd challenged him to earlier either. This time, she'd used a huffy fast walk, as if she wanted to get as far away from him and his questions as possible.

For only the second time in his life, Jeff didn't know what to do for a woman in emotional distress. As a psychologist, he'd sent plenty of patients out of his office after they'd undergone a highly provocative session. But he'd never followed them home, never seen the aftereffects of that session. Normally, by the time a patient returned for the next appointment, his or her mind had processed the information from their last meeting and he or she was prepared to move on.

With April, though, he didn't have the luxury of time and distance. Neither did she.

The dishes clattered in their drainer on the counter, and he looked up from the kindling arrangement in the fireplace in time to see her slam a coffee cup against a plate. Another loud clink rent the air, and he winced. It might be a good idea to get her out of the kitchen before they wound up eating on stoneware splinters tonight.

Unfortunately, the ever-whirring cameras prevented him from simply striding in there and yanking her away from the sink.

"Let's leave the rest of the dishes until later," he called out in as innocuous a tone as he could manage.

"That's okay," she replied, her voice saccharine sweet. "I'd rather do them now. I can't abide a dirty kitchen."

Wow, that went well, didn't it? Next.

"All right. Then I challenge you to that game of Parcheesi you suggested last night."

She looked up from the sink and blew a stray wisp of hair out of her face with pursed lips. "Look, Jeff. I'm kind of busy here at the moment. Why don't you find something to do without me?"

Come to think of it, why didn't he? She was a big girl. She could take care of herself. And a little more space would do them both some good.

"You know, you're right. I'm going for a run." He turned away from the fireplace, leaving the stack of wood unlit.

"Good." Her tone held no interest in his words at all.

"Good," he muttered, and headed into the bedroom to change his clothes.

After stripping out of the sweater and jeans he wore, he stood in his boxers and allowed the cold air to bring down his internal temperature. A run was exactly what he needed to rid his body of the pent-up tension it held.

With luck, by the time he returned, April would have sorted through her feelings regarding their discussion and accepted the troubles in her life she couldn't change right now. If, after she'd cooled down, she wanted to discuss her issues further, he'd be happy to accommodate her. After opening her old scars, the least he could do was allow her the opportunity to re-heal.

Leaving his clothes where they'd fallen, he pulled a pair of sweats and a T-shirt out of his drawer and practically threw them on. He returned to the living room, but April never looked up from the sink.

What was she doing, washing every dish in the cupboard? There were only two of them here. What had they dirtied during lunch? Two plates, two forks, a Thermos, and a bowl. Okay, plus the coffeepot. Still, how long could that take to wash?

Giving in to a childish impulse, he slammed the door as he left.

April waited a good five minutes after the loud boom before she gave up punishing the dishes and strode down the hall to the only room without eyes. With every step, the phrase *Whose darling are you?* echoed in her ears.

Once safe within the bedroom's confines, she locked the door and paced from corner to corner. All the while, she glared at their "wall of Jericho" and fought back tears of frustration with loud sniffs—until she noticed the pile of clothes on the floor.

She remembered her ex-husband's comments regarding how easily she'd win this challenge.

You'll have cameras filming every moment you're living with this self-help guru. Picking up after him, cooking for him, cleaning for him. What better way to prove your point about everyone looking for a mother?

She rolled her eyes toward the ceiling. "Great idea, Peter," she said aloud. "What am I supposed to do if there are no cameras to see me picking up after him? You didn't think this whole thing out fully, did you?"

Apparently, neither had she. Why had she listened to her ex about this Harmony House game in the first place?

Easy.

Habit. From the day they'd met in tenth-grade chemistry class, she'd given in to his every whim, believing herself lucky to have such a fantastic-looking guy interested in her. But in the end, where had it left her? Divorced, broke, and lonely—and stuck here.

As much as reality stung, she had to face one undeniable fact. Jeff's analysis session on the knoll opened her eyes to the mistakes she'd made since her turbulent adolescence.

When she really considered everything, she saw that her entire life was a catalog of approval-seeking at all costs. Always too unsure to make a decision on her own, she'd allowed others to lead her where they wanted—first her mother, then Peter. Even Rainey-Day-Wife had come into being because Ed Kingsley had approached *her.* She'd never had an original idea in her whole rotten, miserable life.

Just once, she'd like to recall a time when she didn't crumble under pressure from an outsider. Unfortunately, no matter how she twisted her brain, she couldn't come up with one instance in which she hadn't allowed someone else to make a decision for her.

She'd been too complacent, too wishy-washy, too stupid to realize that her opinion was the only one that mattered. All her problems existed because she let them happen. From Becky's conception to this Harmony House fiasco, every stupid misstep had come about when she'd kowtowed to someone else instead of her own conscience.

And now she was making the same mistake with Jeff. Well, not exactly the same mistake. She hadn't kowtowed to Jeff—yet. Then again, she'd come awfully close when he'd leaned toward her during their picnic.

What had happened to the sane April out there on the bluff? Why on earth had she believed he planned to kiss her? And why

was she so disappointed he hadn't? Where had her resolve to remain impassive to his charms gone?

She needed constantly to remind herself he was the enemy in
this game. One day's niceties, one cup of coffee in bed and she'd
thrown away every promise she'd made to withstand his acts of
consideration and prove that her theories were closer to the truth
than his.

Unfortunately, she hadn't counted on how powerful those simple
acts of consideration could be. Maybe if she'd been exposed to
them a little more often before now, they might not mean so much.
Yet another truth she'd faced during their talk this afternoon:
despite the passage of time, that teenager in the kitchen, hearing
her mother crush her spirits with a thoughtless remark, still resided
inside her. And the smallest kindness from any source helped build
up what Mommie Dearest had torn down that night.

On top of her other issues, she hadn't spent any real time with
a man since the dissolution of her marriage six years earlier. At
first, she'd had no interest. Then she'd had no time.

Time to take stock of your current predicament, April, my girl.

Okay, so she had some major issues with low self-esteem. But
she also had two kids to care for and a business to protect. She
could tough out this month. Jutting her chin in the air, she forced
her doubts into her brain's basement. She would not let Jeff's
proximity affect her in any way.

So Jeff had thick, gorgeous hair she itched to run her fingers
through. So it sat atop the head and profile of a Greek god. So he
had shoulders as broad as Wyoming. And it was all packaged in a
runner's body. *Yummy.*

Yes, yummy, but was that any reason to turn into a mindless
puddle of goo anytime the man glanced her way? After all, she
wasn't a needy teenager anymore. She was a grown woman. And
for all his good looks and yummy physique, Jeff had some Nean-
derthal opinions about a grown woman's place in the modern
world, opinions that clashed dramatically with the life she'd made
for herself.

Independence is the greatest gift we're given in life.

Repeating the mantra in her head, she picked up his sweater

and jeans. The clove scent that clung to the garments wafted on the air, and she inhaled deeply before folding the articles and placing them on his bed.

When she turned, she came face-to-face with the wall of Jericho. And an overwhelming need surged through her.

With renewed resolve, she shoved the makeshift curtain out of the way and strode to her side of the room. Where exactly had she hidden her special pick-me-up box? Her "just in case" scenario had suddenly become necessity.

Whether she indulged her impulse to escape reality or to find some artificial fortitude didn't matter. She became everywoman, taking out her frustrations on men who thought they knew all a woman's secrets.

She found the box buried beneath a pile of sweaters and pulled it out. With her precious possession clutched to her chest, she dipped her head to inhale the sweet, heady fragrance. The scent alone stiffened her spine and cleared her murky brain cells. She strode to the bathroom and carefully locked the door behind her.

When she turned the tap on the tub, a guilty squeal rang through the tiled room. Her shoulders hunched, and she winced, waiting for some reaction from beyond the door.

Nothing.

Apparently, Jeff was still out of the house. Perfect.

As hot water filled the tub and steamed the air, she sat on the closed toilet and flipped open the lid of her special box. She pulled out the bubble bath first—milk and honey, her favorite—followed by the matching body lotion, the pedicure kit, the deep conditioner for her hair, and the mud mask. *Let the pampering begin.*

One of Bette Davis' most famous lines popped into her head and she uttered it aloud. "Fasten your seat belts. It's going to be a bumpy night."

An hour later, April had indulged her skin with a long, sweet soak. Her hair gleamed, thanks to the deep conditioner and plastic wrap she'd worn during her bath. Her fingers and toes sported Petal Pretty polish on their nails.

Despite her homemade spa treatment, however, when Jeff finally stepped inside again, her spirits sank. Who knew a man could look so good at his worst?

Jeff's dark glossy hair now shimmered with sweat. His shirt lay plastered against his chest. Beneath the wet cloth, those delicious hills and valleys were finally revealed in all their glory. At least she'd been right about one thing. His upper body was a chiseled landscape of perfection. Carved pecs rose up and down in a syncopated rhythm as he panted for breath.

"I need a shower," he murmured as he stumbled past her toward the bathroom.

That was it? No "What smells so nice?" or "Gee, your hair looks so shiny"?

She tiptoed closer, brushing her bare feet against the Pergo floor to draw attention to her perfect pink pedicure.

"Holler if you need me," she murmured in her best Lauren Bacall voice.

At last, he stopped at the entrance to the hallway and stared, his gaze scanning her from head to toe. "Did you change your clothes?"

"No." Satisfaction rippled through her veins.

"Are you sure? You look different somehow."

She forced a lighthearted laugh. "I'm sure I'd remember if I'd changed my clothes in the last hour."

"Yeah, I guess you would, wouldn't you?" he replied, and walked down the hallway.

The minute she heard the bathroom door close, she fluffed her hair and smiled.

Subtle, but he *had* noticed. And that was enough for her—for now.

The shower's needling spray pounded against Jeff's flesh, reviving life in his exhausted muscles.

What exactly had April done in his absence? As sure as he knew his name, he knew she'd changed something about herself. Beneath the recessed lighting in the kitchen ceiling, her hair had sparked like wildfire. And the air around her smelled—for lack of a better word—*delicious*. No way would he have been able to sit at a dining room table or on a blanket outside and eat lunch with that tantalizing aroma lingering nearby.

More interesting to him than what she'd done was why she'd bothered. Clearly, this change in her meant something important.

One lesson he'd learned during his marriage: women often used appearance as a weapon. If a husband and wife had a fight, the man might head to a local bar or work out in a gym to blow off steam. The woman went shopping or got a haircut. Her self-esteem gained a boost if she found a way to look better.

He nearly slapped his forehead as realization struck hard. Of course. During their insightful discussion about her family, her ego had taken a tremendous beating. She must have spent their time apart prettying herself up to confirm she still held control over her life.

Well, he'd play along—pay lots of attention to her, shower her with compliments, and make her feel better about herself. He'd even cook dinner for her tonight. Then maybe she'd smile again.

Not that he cared if she smiled, he told himself as he turned off the water and stepped out of the tub. He only hoped her improved mood would demonstrate that his book's methods worked.

Her happiness would mean nothing to him if it weren't for the cameras recording in the other rooms and the audience's reaction to what showed up on their televisions at home. His desire to brighten her mood had nothing to do with any attraction on his part.

Keeping April happy merely made their living together easier.

Chapter Thirteen

April sat across the polished cherry dining table from Jeff, a steaming dish of beef burgundy before her. A goblet of red wine stood on one side of her plate, a glass of water on the other. She never touched her wine throughout the meal, favoring the cold, clear liquid.

Lit candelabra served as a barrier between them, separating their faces as well as their figures. April welcomed the distance, since it helped ease the nervous flutters in her stomach and allowed her to swallow the beef and water without choking.

Somehow, she'd pictured an entirely different scenario when she'd pulled out her little spa kit. She wanted him to notice the change in her appearance, which he did. But she also wanted him to wonder, to stare at her with curiosity, to imagine why any man in his right mind would leave her. Instead, he fawned over her to the point where she wriggled in her chair and her skin itched.

Unfortunately, after his shower, he'd returned to the living room, fully clothed and smelling better and spicier than her favorite Tex-Mex meal. He announced that he planned to make dinner tonight and threw her out of the kitchen to "relax for a while."

Three hours later, she still couldn't relax. Her mind refused to cooperate, torturing *her* rather than her intended victim. Every time he smiled, or even locked his gaze on her face, flames consumed her from head to toe. The candlelight only enhanced the silver glint in his eyes.

In the meantime, her companion played the smooth courtier with grace, never once showing any sign of unease. Well, yeah, sure. He probably dated supermodels and Hollywood's elite, not some hausfrau–slash–high school dropout from Nowhereville.

"You look very pretty tonight."

His comment couldn't make a dent in her self-deprecation, and she snorted.

"Do you know your eyes are the exact shade of warmed honey on toast?"

Huh? Should she take that as a compliment? "Thank you," she murmured, and stared at the dancing flames on the candlesticks.

Doubts about his sincerity niggled at her brain. Jeff had gone out of his way to be attentive, accommodating, and full of compliments tonight. She didn't buy the act for a minute.

He probably thinks I'll forget to ask him about his personal life if he keeps showering me with empty phrases like "warmed honey on toast."

No way, José. As she took another sip of water, she looked at him over the rim of the glass. It was time to up the ante.

"I believe it's your turn in the hot seat. Tell me about your family."

"Not much to tell," he said with a noncommittal shrug.

She placed the glass on the table and leaned back against her chair. "I'll be the judge of that, if you don't mind. Are your parents alive?"

He nodded, as if subtly agreeing to her interview techniques. "They're alive, but I almost never see them these days. Dad retired about five years ago, and my parents travel extensively. They're rarely in this country anymore. Instead, they'll call me from a junk in Hong Kong one week, the Egyptian pyramids the next. Last month, I got a postcard from the Australian outback."

"That's so wonderful." She propped her head on her fist and indulged the fantasy of world travel. Heck, she'd settle for Disney World travel. "My parents never got the opportunity to enjoy retirement together."

"Maybe not, but my mother would give up all her adventures to have just one of the gifts your mother has."

"Oh?" She arched a brow. "And what gifts would those be?"

"Grandchildren."

She grabbed her glass and gulped the last of the water to cool her flesh. Lord, when had the room become so warm? Maybe she should shift her chair farther away from the fire. But then, that would put her closer to Jeff. Out of the frying pan . . .

After placing the empty glass against her cheek, she managed to say, "So your parents are well-adjusted, normal people. Do you have any siblings?"

"I have an older sister. She's divorced, no children. Her baby is the family corporation. When Dad left, my sister naturally stepped in as president of the contracting business."

"Naturally? As opposed to you?"

"Mmm-hmm. Lauren was pretty much raised to inherit the position. Since she was about five, she spent all her time following my father around the company. Dad even had a smaller version of his desk built and installed in his office for her. After high school, she went on to college, majoring in business. She graduated from Wharton, then worked in every department we have so she'd know the ins and outs of the corporation as a whole. She served as chief financial officer for three years before Dad retired."

"Does it bother you that she's running the company and you're not?"

Finished with his meal, he placed his knife and fork atop the plate and pushed them to one side. "No. I never wanted the company. I like what I do and could never give it up. Lauren is much more suited to take Dad's place than I'll ever be. She's a real barracuda." He grinned, craning his neck to smile at the camera overhead. "But I mean that in a good way, of course."

"Tell me about your wife."

He whirled to face April, his expression somber. Perhaps the flickering flames caused an optical illusion, but she could have sworn his eyes glistened. Then he blinked, twice in rapid succession, and the shimmer disappeared.

"There's even less to tell there," he said, but he bit off each word.

Yeah, sure. And I'm the Princess of Peoria.

"I'll tell you what," she said. "Why don't you tell me one thing about your wife that used to infuriate you, and I'll tell you one of Peter's quirks that drove me crazy."

He shook his head. "I don't think so."

"Oh, come on. It doesn't have to be some deep, dark secret."

His eyebrows rose in questioning arcs. "What makes you think Emma had a deep, dark secret?"

"I don't think that at all. As a matter of fact, I really don't want to know any deep secrets if she *did* have them. Poking around in the dark is your area of expertise." She wiped her mouth and balled her napkin beside her plate. "Look, I'm not writing an exposé for the tabloids or anything. I'm only trying to make conversation. Tell me something humorous and interesting. One of those quirks you originally found enchanting that grated on your nerves after you were married for a while. It could be as simple as 'She drank milk out of the carton while standing naked in front of the refrigerator,' or 'She always wore socks to bed because her feet were like twin blocks of ice.'"

He blinked. "Why on earth would you want to know something like that?"

"Because it's interesting to me." She nodded toward the camera mounted behind him. "And it's interesting to *them.* We all knew Emma Prentiss the soap star. You were one of the few fortunate people to know the real Emma Prentiss. I'd like you to share a piece of that with me. With us."

"She was allergic to cats."

"I don't want her medical history," she retorted. "I want something personal. Something that made her human, full of idiosyncrasies, and totally lovable. Here. I'll give you an example. My ex, Peter, is a great exterminator—one of the best in his company, actually." She giggled. "But he's scared to death of spiders. I mean, literally paralyzed at the sight of a web. Can you imagine? A man who makes his living scrambling around attics, construction sites, and on the floors of buildings, killing all sorts of creepy crawlies, and he's afraid of a little spider? At first it was cute, you know? Every time he found a spider in the house, he'd yell for me to get rid of it. After the first six months, though, when he continually shouted for me while I was in the shower, on the phone, or feeding an infant, that little eccentricity lost its charm."

His lips twitched as he fought back a smile, and she pushed her advantage. "Now your turn. Tell me something about Emma."

He leaned back in his chair to stare at the ceiling while rubbing his temples with his fingertips. Time crawled. Had she pushed him too far?

Finally, he placed his hands on the table and sighed. "Okay. I don't know if this is as good as your spider story, but here goes. I met Emma when I was in college, and I once confessed that the one thing I missed about home was a quality meal. My normal dinner in those days consisted of boxed macaroni and cheese."

April laughed. "The kids and I had a few months like that when Peter first left us. At a dollar a box, it was the cheapest dinner available. So what happened?"

"Well, a few days later, Emma invited me over to her apartment for dinner. The food was phenomenal. We started with a lemongrass soup, continued through a fabulous beef Wellington with new potatoes and carrots au gratin, and finished with raspberry chocolate mousse."

He smiled and licked his lips, and April resisted the urge to do the same at the imagined taste of such a meal.

"It was the one and only time she ever cooked for me while we dated. During our honeymoon, I dropped a lot of hints about that dinner, anticipating the wondrous food she would create in the gourmet kitchen our apartment contained. She always answered with something like 'I'm sure you'll be surprised.' "

"And were you?"

"Oh, I was surprised all right. On our first day back, I came home after work, appetite whetted for a culinary masterpiece. A fireman met me at the entrance to our apartment. Emma had set the kitchen towels on fire, trying to cook one of those boil-in-a-bag dinners."

April's jaw dropped. "She couldn't cook?"

He shook his head, his smile broadening.

"What about that fabulous meal she made while you were dating?"

"She had her parents' personal chef come to her apartment and cook the whole thing. He hid in the linen closet while I was there."

Laughter poured from her lips, a river of mirth. "Oh, Jeff, I'm sorry, but to imagine some stiff-backed, snotty chef stuffed into a closet while you sat there dining on his hard work and complimenting someone else. It's too funny."

Jeff laughed with her. "I learned to cook to keep her away from the stove, as a matter of self-preservation."

"I'll bet. Not to mention fire prevention. Smokey the Bear would be proud."

When his laughter subsided, Jeff looked at the woman across from him with newfound respect. April had just accomplished something no one had been able to do in years. She'd allowed him a chance to remember Emma with fondness and joy—not with remorse, guilt, or anger. *The good times,* well-meaning strangers often called them.

"What?" she asked, shattering his reverie.

"What 'what'?"

"You're looking at me funny."

"I am?" He broke off the stare. "I'm sorry. I was thinking of something else."

"Oh." Her face filled with pink color, and her gaze dropped to her empty plate. "I guess I'll start clearing the table."

Oops. Not smart, Jeff. You don't tell a woman you're thinking about something else while staring at her.

He placed a hand on her wrist. "No, you don't. Cleaning up is my job. I told you. I'm in charge of tonight's feast. Go sit near the fire and relax. In fact, why don't you grab a board game and set it up over there while I take care of this mess? Once I whip the dishes into shape, I'll whip your butt at Parcheesi."

Her eyes narrowed. "You think you can?"

"Of course I can," he replied, and nodded toward the ruby liquid in the glass to the right of her plate. "Take your wine with you."

She screwed her lips into a moue. "If you insist."

"You don't like Shiraz?"

As if hoping to appease him, she lifted the goblet and sipped the wine. The screwy face remained. "I guess I'm just not much of a wine drinker."

"Or maybe you don't know the proper way to drink it."

Chapter Fourteen

Chucka-chucka-chucka. Scriiiiitch.

She'd rolled boxcars. Jeff hid a smile while April stared at the pair of dice sitting on the Parcheesi board. Deep concentration etched her forehead as she considered her next move. Decisions, decisions. Should she send his man back to the start circle or push her own man closer to home? Or she could take a new man out, if she so desired.

A full minute passed, and Jeff shook his head. She was taking the game far too seriously, as if the fate of the free world relied on her four blue men making it home before his red guys got there. Someone should remind her that this was only a game—a distraction. And since he was the only "someone" around, the responsibility fell to him.

A stray curl drifted before her eyes, and Jeff seized the opportunity afforded him. One slow exhale of breath from his pursed lips sent the thin wad of hair back into place, simultaneously breaking her concentration.

She looked up, her hand on a blue playing piece, and frowned at him.

"What?" he asked with a shrug.

"You know what. You're trying to distract me."

His smile disappeared and his eyes widened, conveying newborn innocence. "Oh, now that's not true. If I wanted to distract you, I'd lean over like this." He propped himself up on his elbows and stretched his length across the table until only mingled breath separated their faces. "Then, I'd do something completely outrageous. Like this."

Before she could figure out his intentions, he placed a kiss square on the tip of her pert, freckled nose. She gasped as if he'd splashed ice water on her face, and pulled back from the table, her eyelashes fluttering against bright pink cheeks.

"Wh-why did you do that?"

He had no idea. But he'd gotten a lot of enjoyment from the sudden action. And not just because of the element of surprise either. Something about April's intensity begged for kisses of distraction. He couldn't quite put his finger, or his lips, on what it was.

Certainly the softness of her skin and that rose-pink blush donated to the cause. And the way she looked at him—like he was part superhero and part villain—made him want to play both roles. If he'd had a mustache, he'd have twirled it and cackled with delight.

Still, April had more to recommend her than a colorful face and tempting vulnerability. He couldn't explain how she affected him, nor could he squelch the urge to kiss her again, maybe this time on her cheek before he moved downward to her lower jaw and that long graceful column of neck.

Then she smiled at him. "I suppose you thought such an outrageous action would sidetrack me and gain you an advantage."

"You think so?"

"Of course." She rolled her eyes in an exaggerated expression of patience. "Boys will be boys."

By God, he was no boy, and he wouldn't allow her to mistake him for one. For the rest of this game, he planned to use every trick in his arsenal to fluster her and keep that blush burning in her cheeks.

He began slowly. A long sip of red wine while his eyes focused, unblinking, on her lips the entire time. When he gave her a slow wink over the edge of the glass, her blush deepened and spread to both ears. *Ah, sweet victory.*

Hiding a smile, he picked up his cup of dice and rolled them onto the board. A three and a four. He licked his fingertip and traced it along his lower lip before moving one of his men the requisite seven steps.

The blush moved across the bridge of her nose, to the very place his lips had touched only seconds earlier. Satisfied, he picked up his dice to return them to his cup, but accidentally brushed against her wrist as she reached for her own cup. At the simple contact, her mouth opened in a wide o. He couldn't stop the idea that came to mind.

One quick sip of wine, and he pressed his mouth against hers, transferring the warm, spicy liquid into her mouth. She yanked away from him so quickly the game pieces scattered across the board and onto the floor. While he bit back his laughter, she stared at him aghast, her eyes tearing.

"Swallow it, silly," he ordered.

Her neck bobbed when she did as he instructed.

"It's good, right?"

"Mmm-hmm," she said, her doe eyes fixed on him in wonder.

"There, see? I told you that you didn't know the proper way to drink red wine."

She gave no reply. She merely sat across from him, transfixed, her hand holding an empty dice cup.

Hoping to break the spell, he glanced away and immediately saw the lens of the camera peeking at him from the mantel.

How could he have forgotten about their continual-surveillance friends? A hint of resentment brewed in the pit of his stomach and mingled with the wine he'd drunk, to form a pool of burning acid.

Tomorrow morning, in front of a nationwide audience, Grant and Jocelyn would dissect ulterior motives for his little wine trick. What kind of excuse could he possibly come up with to explain this nonsense? Especially when he didn't have a reasonable excuse to tell himself.

The moment Jeff's lips closed over hers, a whoosh roared through April's ears. Then a sweet, pungent liquid filled her mouth. Blood? No. As the liquid danced and fizzled over her taste buds, she realized he'd transferred the wine in his mouth to hers. The idea left her breathless.

As awareness filtered into her senses, panic seized her, and she pushed away with all the force her limp body could muster. She wanted to gasp, but the wine inside her cheeks prevented her from forming a sound.

"Swallow it, silly," he'd said, so she had.

Unlike the sweet white zinfandel April normally sipped, this wine had a stronger aftertaste and a thicker consistency. But she couldn't deny she liked the taste. Or did Jeff's bizarre method of exchanging the beverage add to the flavor? No answer came to her.

Confusion muddled her thoughts. All she wanted now was escape, a quick retreat before she surrendered.

"Excuse me," she murmured, and fled the room.

"April?" Jeff called after her, but she didn't stop.

She raced into the bedroom and hid behind their wall of Jericho. She peeled off her clothes and slipped into her bedtime sweats in three seconds flat—a new world record. After sliding under the covers, she stared at the ceiling.

Minutes ticked by before Jeff's sigh signaled his entrance. Did he sigh with disappointment or relief? She couldn't tell and didn't want to know.

"April?" he said tentatively.

She stiffened, closed her eyes, and silently begged sleep to overcome her.

"Okay, fine," he said. "Have it your way."

She heard his movements on the other side of the room but refused to open her eyes until the light clicked off.

In the darkness, April tossed and turned, knowing she faced another sleepless night. She concentrated her thoughts on her children, her home, her business—even her ex-husband—in an attempt to cool her burning lips. She'd think of anything that would keep her mind from pondering Jeff's kiss and his reasoning.

Worse than his action, however, her reaction scared the bejesus out of her. She'd never in her life felt such an incredible pull toward a man. It was as if he were a gorgeous magnet and she was made of steel.

Just before she gave in to fatigue, her mind's eye focused on the black camera mounted above the fireplace mantel, which recorded every moment with clarity. And April knew that sleep would never come for her again.

Chapter Fifteen

W hy don't you tell us about that kiss, April?" Jocelyn's catty voice purred through her earpiece. *Meow, meow.*

April's face heated to the temperature of the sun's surface. Why were they asking *her*? She was the kissee, not the kisser. They should be asking Jeff to explain it.

She cast pleading eyes in his direction, but he never moved a muscle. Apparently, he didn't plan to jump into this fray. Panic reigned in her head for a full minute. No one would come to her rescue. Once again, she was on her own.

Quick, April. Buy time.

"What exactly do you want to know, Jocelyn?"

"Well, for starters," Jocelyn purred, "what's Dr. Jeff like as a kisser?"

The audience cheered their appreciation of the question.

Frazzled nerve endings crackled in April's veins, and she turned fully in her seat to seek Jeff's assistance. He offered her a careless shrug and a smile full of unmitigated pride. The son of a gun had the nerve to enjoy her discomfort! Well, if Jeff refused to help her, maybe Bette Davis would.

"It was a man's last desperate stand at superintendency."

That erased the smile from Jeff's face.

Thank you, Bette.

"But surely you felt something, April," Jocelyn persisted. "I should imagine such a sweet kiss made the wine taste better."

"Actually, I found the wine too dry for my liking."

Was there an exorcist in the house? Bette Davis' spirit suddenly possessed April, and she couldn't control what came out of her mouth. The audience's response lowered in tone and volume, as if in reflection of the insult she'd paid Jeff.

"Jeff," Jocelyn piped up. "What do you think about April's comments?"

April dared a sideways glance in his direction. She expected his anger, or at least a quick retort, but he merely smiled and inched a little closer on the couch.

"I think her memory needs refreshing," he said.

Before she could form a reply, his mouth covered hers. She heard the audience's roar of approval, then nothing but her heart's furious pounding in her ears. The cameras around them, the giant spotlight in her face, the crewmen gawking from the sidelines, and smarmy David all disappeared in a blur of colors and mishmashed lines.

This was not the simple kiss and transfer of wine from last night. This was all-consuming, like being swept into a tornado and whirled round and round at Mach 1.

Her hands gripped Jeff's shoulders, clinging to those sturdy supports with all their might, drawing him closer, nearer, inside her, breath by breath. Every pore of her skin reached for contact with him.

When his tongue ran along her lips, she shivered. He pulled her closer into his embrace, enveloping her in the heat of his arms. No longer an individual, she became an extension of Jeff. His hand was her hand; his lips were her lips. His heart thundered inside her chest and echoed the rapid rhythm of her own. But she couldn't break away if she tried—not that she wanted to try. She'd rather feed her fingertips to an alligator than lose this connection.

Unfortunately, Jeff didn't seem to experience the same twister of emotions. First he removed her arms from around his neck. Then he gently pushed her away. The moment her lips lost touch with his, reality returned.

She looked into his bemused face, and utter humiliation stole her senses.

"Wow, Jeff, April." Grant Harrison's voice invaded her eardrums. "That was quite an exhibition you two put on. April, do you wish to change your opinion of Jeff's kiss now?"

"Huh?" What was Grant talking about? Her brain refused to resurface.

Grant chuckled. "I'll take that as a yes."

"So will I," Jeff added.

The audience burst into a chorus of laughter that rang in April's ears. She sat on the couch, dumbfounded. What was so funny? Where had her sanity gone?

The interview came to an end a few minutes later—minutes lost on April.

She woke up only when David offered his traditional "Good work, guys. See ya tomorrow," and exited the house with his crew.

Her temper reached the boiling point when she saw the reason for her discomfort smiling as if today's show had aired without a hitch.

Why, you . . . You . . .

He kissed her! Dr. Jeff kissed April! On the air!

A stunned Summer clicked off the television and placed the remote control in its cradle on her smoked-glass cocktail table.

Why hadn't April said anything? Done anything? After Dr. Jeff kissed her, she just kind of sat there, this dumb look on her face. If she liked it, she could've smiled. If she didn't, she could've slapped him. Instead, she did nothing for the rest of the segment.

No wonder Peter had left her. Summer suddenly wondered if her ex-brother-in-law's roving eye had something to do with her sister's lackluster reaction to passion. Really, it was none of her business. But the voice in the back of her head, the voice growing louder and louder every day, trumpeted.

April's reticence could easily be the reason for her husband's faithlessness. But what's your excuse?

Words continued to fail April when Jeff rose from the couch.

The insipid grin never leaving his insipid face, Jeff headed for the kitchen. "What should we do for lunch today?"

"I'm not hungry," she answered as she strode to the closet. "As a matter of fact, I'm going out for a little while."

"Out where?" Jeff followed her.

She slipped her jacket onto her shoulders. "Just out. I need some air."

"I'll go with you," he offered, reaching for his jacket.

"No, thanks. I want to be alone."

Sensing he might argue, she flung open the front door and raced outside. The door slammed noisily behind her, but she didn't care.

Let him analyze *that*.

She stepped onto the porch and allowed the brisk air to cool her feverish mood. But before she could reach 98.6 degrees again, the front door's creak told her Jeff hadn't acquiesced to her demand after all, no matter how succinctly she'd voiced her preferences.

"Would you care to explain what set you off?" he asked, closing the door behind him.

He didn't look at her. He kept his gaze on the mountains in the distance, as if she weren't worth his notice. Frustration heated the air.

Even if he didn't see her expression, he must have *felt* the anger emanating from her, crackling in the air like summer lightning.

"You made me look like an idiot," she snapped.

At last, he turned to stare at her, his expression incredulous. "Why? Because I kissed you?"

"You didn't just kiss me. You kissed me until I was handicapped."

The moment the words left her lips, she wished she could take them back. It was too late.

Jeff folded his arms over his chest, a posture of overweening pride. "I handicapped you? No one's ever accused me of that before."

"You know what I mean." Unable to look into his grin without kissing him or slapping him, she turned her attention to the mountains in the distance. "You caught me completely off guard, and I couldn't think straight after that."

"Would it make you feel any better if I said you handicapped me too?"

"No." *Wait.* She gaped at him. "I did?"

"Yes, you did. I haven't kissed a woman since . . . well, let's just say in a long time." He shrugged. "I haven't had the inclination. Of course, I'd forgotten what a pleasant pastime it could be."

"I've never kissed anyone but my husband," she confessed in a tone barely above a whisper.

One eyebrow arched at her. "Never?"

"Well, I've kissed my parents and relatives. But romantically . . . no, I've never kissed anyone but Peter." Surrendering to her embarrassment, she dropped her head and watched her feet shuffle along the floorboards. "We met when I was fifteen. I never dated anyone else."

"Not even after the divorce?"

"After the divorce, the last thing I wanted was to give *another* man control over me."

"I can understand that." His shadow moved across the floor as he rocked on his heels. "Looks like we're both out of practice then, huh?"

The wind picked up, and she rubbed some of the chill from her arms. "I guess so."

"Do you think we should practice a little more? Without the cameras this time?"

She stopped rubbing and looked up in surprise. "Are you asking permission to kiss me again?"

Now *he* glanced at *his* shuffling feet. "Well, yeah. I guess I am. What do you say? May I kiss you?"

Should she let him? Did she dare?

A thrill of anticipation rippled through her bones. He'd asked permission. No one had ever asked permission to kiss her before. The originality of his proposal tempted her to give in. Yet she held back.

What exactly did she feel for Jeff? It couldn't be love; she'd known him only a few days. Love took longer to blossom. Heck, a tomato plant took longer to blossom.

Lust was probably closer to the truth.

April had had some experience with lust—not in eighteen years or so, but she still remembered how her last surrender to that deadly sin had affected the rest of her life. She'd always excused that mistake with the notion she'd been young and naïve when she fell for Peter's clumsy declarations of eternal love on her parents' couch.

But she was supposed to be older and wiser now—too old and too wise to succumb to her body's desire for a momentary passionate connection.

Besides, she couldn't trust him. What if this was all part of his campaign of "infinite acts of love and consideration"? No matter how smooth his attempts, she didn't dare fall for them.

"April?" Jeff prompted.

"Give me a minute. I'm thinking."

"What's there to think about? Do you want to kiss me or not?"

"Oh, I *want* to kiss you, Jeff. I'm not so sure I should, though."

He moved closer, so close his breath wafted against her cheek, and his cologne tickled her nostrils. "Is that a no, then?"

Her heart skipped a beat. "I guess so."

Chicken.

Chapter Sixteen

In April's experience, nothing cooled passion's fire more effectively than scrubbing a toilet. So after she left Jeff on the porch with a lost-puppy expression, she strode inside, determined to clean every crevice of Harmony House.

Later that evening, she collapsed into bed, exhausted from her toil, but feeling pretty darn proud of herself. With housework as an excuse, she'd managed to avoid any proximity to Jeff and gain some control over her waxing libido.

Why did her body's perceptions choose this month, of all times, to become acutely aware of the sensuality all around her? Why did cool sheets create delicious shivers on satiny skin in the darkness?

She'd barely survived another torturous dinner tonight. Seeing Jeff's lips close over his fork reminded April of the sweet pressure of his mouth on hers and the red wine passing between them. She thought of how the spicy liquid had fizzled on her tongue and slid with ease down her throat, spreading heat into her belly.

Kicking off the covers, she allowed the icy night air to freeze the bonfire that crackled in her veins. Goose bumps rippled across her flesh, the first honest reaction her body had stimulated all day—and one with an easy explanation.

A rustle from the other side of the suspended sheet forced her attention back to Jeff's proximity. She'd almost become accustomed to the subtle scent of his aftershave following her everywhere during the day. Yet each night her heartbeat accelerated and her breath caught in her lungs when she considered that a skimpy cotton sheet and roughly ten feet barred her from him. Sometimes—now, for example—the distance seemed more like inches.

For some strange reason, his nearness reminded her of the closet monsters she used to battle for Michael every night. Spray bottle filled with "monster juice" in hand, April would tiptoe around her son's room, spritzing the air to banish the nightmare beasties who waited behind coats and shoes to creep out in the dark and frighten him. For the longest time, Michael kept the spray bottle next to his bed while he slept—in case she'd missed one.

So where was her bottle of monster juice now? Nowhere nearby. If she'd had that special brew with her, she'd have sprayed the stuff all over herself and the house to banish the monster, Jeff, on Day One. Talk about giving her nightmares . . .

Their discussion about her family's quirks had certainly battered her ego into a pulpy mess. She chewed her lower lip and considered how all those confessions also provided Jeff a whole new set of weapons to use against her to win this competition . . . or reality show . . . or whatever the producers wanted to call this farce.

Well, she thought with one last glare at their makeshift wall, she'd steel herself to remain immune to any of his barbs, no matter how disarming he tried to make them. She'd clam up and not speak about her personal life again. She'd take Peter's advice and transfer all her righteous anger to Jeff. He could represent her mother, her sister, and her ex-husband in one package.

One hot-kissing, tempting package . . .

No. She wouldn't think about that. Fists clenched to fight the ache that spread up from her belly, she stared at a cluster of stars through the skylight. Out here in the country, they burned brighter than they did at home. Less air pollution, she supposed.

No wonder Brooklyn loved living in the mountains. Maybe when this challenge ended, she'd take the kids to her sister's b-and-b for an extended vacation. Another few weeks, and ski season, along with the multitude of tourists the sport brought, would arrive. Becky and Mike would love the break from their usual humdrum routine, and Lyn, with her razor-sharp wit and down-to-earth attitude, would help April put all this nonsense into perspective. Yup, that was exactly what she would do—as soon as she won this challenge.

Once April had forced her personal demons under control, her mind flipped to a make-believe calendar. With a curl of her fingers, she made a check mark in the air above her head. She'd survived another day at Harmony House. What would tomorrow bring?

More innuendo and catty remarks from Jocelyn and Grant, of course. At least she could thank God no one had heard the conversation she and Jeff had held on the porch. David's production team would have had a field day twisting Jeff's unusual yet chivalrous request. She shivered at the thought and hugged herself to calm the prickles on her arms. Why had he asked to kiss her, anyway? Was it, as he'd said, that she'd handicapped him the way he'd handicapped her? Or did he have a more sinister goal in mind?

She shook her head. Jeff certainly had a way of putting her on the defensive, didn't he? In the movie *The Cabin in the Cotton,* Bette Davis told Richard Barthelmess, "I'd love to kiss you, but I just washed my hair."

Thinking about that line now, April sighed in disappointment. Why couldn't she have come up with some witty repartee when Jeff had asked to kiss *her?*

"April?"

At her name, she scrambled for the covers to pull them back up. He must have heard her sigh and realized she hadn't fallen asleep yet.

She had to constantly remind herself to stay on her guard around him. Relaxing muscles that had involuntarily stiffened at his voice, she feigned a casual tone. "Hmm?"

"You okay?"

"Uh-huh," she lied. "Just wondering what might be in store for us tomorrow."

"Don't even think about it."

His voice, husky by day, took on an even sultrier quality at night. She could almost feel his hot breath against the crook of her neck. Her internal bonfire blazed anew, and her stomach muscles clenched.

Closing her eyes, she envisioned him beside her on some tropical beach, one finger lazily tracing the curve of her hip while his mouth rained kisses across her throat. Her back arched in tune with the illusion, and a low groan escaped her lips.

"You keep torturing yourself and you'll never get to sleep."

Ka-blam! Jeff's mild censure blasted her fantasy into shards of colorful ice. Awareness returned full force, with a healthy dose of embarrassment. Good Lord, she'd groaned aloud. Did he know where her imagination had taken her in those few seconds?

"Don't worry. We'll practice what we should say tomorrow morning before David shows up," he said. "That seems to work well for us."

Okay, so he obviously thought she'd groaned while thinking about their interview tomorrow. She could live with that kind of misconception. In fact, to further his assumption, she asked, "Do you have any idea what they'll choose to throw at us next?"

"Not offhand. It's a good thing there are no cameras on the porch, though, huh?"

"Funny, I was thinking the very same thing," she admitted. "I could just imagine what kind of fun they'd have with that."

"Well, stop letting your imagination get the best of you."

That was wise advice. Now if only her imagination would listen.

To April's delight, the production team chose to showcase her cleaning spree in the next day's interview. Although she couldn't see the video, the peppy background music and laughter from the audience suggested they'd pieced together her activities and used some sort of flash-cut effect. Her vivid imagination filled in the blanks: her arms and legs windmilling at hyperspeed as she whirled around Harmony House like the cartoon Tasmanian Devil.

"Poor April," Jocelyn purred when the clip ended. "You must have exhausted yourself with all that housework yesterday."

"Not at all." She didn't attempt to stifle the smugness in her tone. "I'm quite accustomed to household chores. After all, it's what my business was founded on."

"And where was Dr. Jeff while you ran yourself in circles?" Grant chimed in.

April dared a glance in Jeff's direction. His furrowed brow spoke volumes, but she merely smiled her triumph at him.

"Gee, I guess I was so busy I didn't notice."

Her earpiece droned with the single sound of a crowd's sympathetic "Awwwww . . ."

She actually had to sit on her hands to keep from rubbing them in glee. For the first time in her life, she experienced the raw power of appreciation. Positive vibes flowed through her as the audience's approval bathed her in a warm glow. If she tried, she knew, right now, she could fly. The heady feeling overwhelmed her, delighted her.

Still, her saner self managed to prevail over the pleasure of the moment. More than ever, she understood Jeff's warning about television getting her soul. In a weak individual, such a high could easily become addictive. And common sense cautioned that the drive to sustain this euphoria could seriously jeopardize her intelligence.

"I was around." Jeff's grumble hurtled her back to earth with the power of gravity. "If April wanted help, she might have asked me. I'm more than willing to do my share of the household chores. I just didn't realize she wanted to do all of them in one day."

April clucked her tongue at him but directed her comments to the audience. "So typical, don't you think, ladies? Men seem to think dishes wash themselves, dust is banished permanently after one swipe with a cloth, and flushing the toilet scrubs it clean."

A faraway "Right on!" resounded from somewhere off mike. *Oh, yes. Right on, indeed.* God, life was good today!

Grant's goofy chuckle in her head had the same effect as nails on a chalkboard, and she suppressed a wince when he said, "Score one point for April."

But Jeff's reaction delighted her more than that of the audience. Nodding, he said softly, "Touché."

"Does this mean you concede already, Dr. Jeff?" Jocelyn asked.

Jeff laughed, but to April, who'd become accustomed to his

spontaneous cheerfulness, the sound rang false. "Of course not. The challenge has only begun. I made a mistake, I admit, but I promise it won't happen again."

April couldn't resist teasing him. From the moment of their first meeting, he'd had her in the hot seat while always maintaining the easygoing posture of the confident one. Well, now he wasn't quite so sure of himself, and she wanted to keep him squirming for as long as possible.

Patting his hand as if to console a child, she said, "Don't worry, Dr. Jeff. Any woman who's been married for a length of time is accustomed to picking up after a man. Somehow, we find the grace to forgive and forget."

He glanced her way, and smoke smoldered in his eyes. Still, he said nothing.

Why not poke him a little harder? "Cat got your tongue, Doctor?"

"Not at all," he replied smoothly. "I'm simply wondering if I should kiss you again so I might get a word in edgewise. It's worked before."

April gasped while an entire zoo full of noise—shrieks and squeals, cackles, hoots, and brays—erupted in her ear.

"And score one point for Dr. Jeff," Jocelyn said with a giggle. "Come on, April. You're not going to let him get away with that threat, are you?"

Talk about a zoo animal . . . Jocelyn's high-pitched twitter could make a hyena cover his ears in disgust. Although tempted to continue the banter with Jeff, April didn't dare rise to the bait— not if he'd sink to kissing her again to win. Her pride couldn't take that kind of abuse a second time.

Why had she admitted that he'd handicapped her with his last kiss? Now he probably planned to fall back on that method whenever she got a leg up on him. Eventually, she'd have to come up with some form of counterattack. At the moment, though, with that stupid red light from the camera fixed on her face, nothing came to mind.

A childhood rhyme sang through her brain: *He who fights and runs away lives to fight another day.*

"I think," she murmured through a quickly tightening throat, "I'll concede this battle."

"No!" Lyn shouted at her television screen. "Come on, April. Don't let him bully you. You're too smart for that."

"I think she likes him," Mrs. Bascomb noted, pointing at April's image with one of her knitting needles.

Mouth agape, Lyn turned to the older woman seated beside her. "No way. April's just stringing him along, letting him win a few battles in the early rounds so she can totally demolish him later."

"If you say so." Mrs. Bascomb tugged at the baby blue yarn ball in the bag at her feet. "She's your sister, so maybe you're right. But she looks pretty flustered to me. You did say she's been without a man in her life since her divorce. And that Dr. Jeff is a real charmer."

"Puh-leez," Lyn retorted. "April's too smart to be taken in by his good looks and smooth maneuvers."

"Maybe she doesn't see it that way," Mrs. Bascomb said with a shrug. "Maybe she's tired of being alone . . . unlike someone else we know."

Lyn shot her a disgruntled look. Mrs. B. had delivered a cheap shot, and they both knew it.

Pasting an angelic expression on her face, the old lady lifted her delicate china cup to her lips and sipped her tea.

"Keep it up," Lyn warned, "and you'll find yourself looking for a comfy chair in another b-and-b."

"Nonsense, sweetheart." She paused in her knitting to hold up the woolen rectangle of traditional pastel baby colors. "Do you know how many of these blankets I've made in the last two years? I keep holding out hope that one day I'll be knitting one for you."

Tears pricked Lyn's eyes, and she lifted her own teacup to hide behind the steamy beverage. "Don't," she managed to say through a rapidly tightening throat. "Please."

Mrs. Bascomb dropped her knitting and patted Lyn's thigh with her gnarled fingers. "Now, Lyn. It's long past time you gave up the ghost and started living again."

The ringing telephone saved Lyn from lashing out at the well-meaning but misguided woman. Wriggling away from Mrs. Bascomb's attempt at comfort, she placed her teacup on the table and reached for the phone.

"Thank you for calling Snowed Inn, your four-season bed-and-breakfast," Lyn intoned. "How may I direct your call?"

"Can you believe she folded so fast?" Summer, on the other end of the line, asked.

While her mind still grappled with Mrs. Bascomb's comments, Lyn's fingers gripped the receiver tight enough to crush it to dust. "No."

"I don't understand what she's doing, do you? First she sat there like a zombie when he kissed her. And now she let him win an argument she had in the bag."

"Mrs. Bascomb thinks April's giving up because she likes him."

"Well, what's not to like?" Summer retorted. "The guy's educated, gorgeous, and so sweet. But honestly, he's not April's type. He might be your type, though."

Lyn sighed. *Not again.* She could not traipse the matchmaking path twice in one afternoon. "Listen, Sum, I have to go. I'm expecting guests today," she lied. "I'll talk to you tomorrow, okay?"

"Okay." Summer's sigh hissed through the receiver. "But listen, Lyn, I really think—"

"Whoops!" Lyn cut her off. "There's their car. Gotta go."

Before Summer could argue, Lyn hung up the phone. But she couldn't silence the grief that raged inside her heart.

Chapter Seventeen

Laundry, old girl. Let's get a load of laundry into the washing machine. Kill two birds with one stone.

More household chores would ice down her hot blood and keep Jeff's lips away from hers. Menial labor would also go a long way toward proving her theory over his. Okay, so maybe she could kill *three* birds.

Rummaging through her hamper, she came up with a few sweaters, some underwear, and three pairs of jeans. *Hmmm.* She might have to reconsider this task. Her sweaters were dry-clean only and her underwear had to be hand washed. Three pairs of jeans did not a load of laundry make. She'd have to do Jeff's clothing as well if she intended to fill the machine. And once again, the cameras wouldn't see her performing something for his benefit.

Unless, of course, she made a production of getting them into the washing machine while in the basement. A camera sat within perfect view down there.

Not bothering to sort them, she scooped up the pile of Jeff's clothes from the hamper on his side of the room and added them to her jeans. The odor of male sweat wafted up to sear her nostrils. Not the little-boy-playing-hard sweat she was used to either, but the more animal scent of a full-grown man.

She hadn't smelled that ripe aroma in years. But she vividly recalled the last time. She'd planned to confront Peter about his infidelity with the company's secretary, her attention focused on more important issues than a disagreeable odor.

She'd suspected his cheating for months but always turned a blind eye to those less-than-discreet indiscretions, to the excuses to work late, the times she couldn't reach him. As women often do, she believed herself somehow responsible for his need to seek affection elsewhere. So she redoubled her efforts to remain appealing to him. She dieted and exercised obsessively, planned romantic dinners, and dressed in lacy lingerie for bed—all to no avail.

Shaking her head, April scattered the memories out of her brain and carried the smelly heap of clothing downstairs. She placed the pile atop the dryer and clicked the washer's dials to cold water, full load.

While the water splashed into the tub, she shook out the clothing, piece by piece, and dropped it inside.

"My jeans," she announced aloud for the camera's benefit. "His jeans. My jeans, his jeans. His socks—oh, ick."

Jeff's socks were damp and rolled into a ball. She'd have to stick her hand inside to pull them straight out. When she slid her fingers into the first one, a sharp intake of breath hissed through her teeth at the clammy feeling of the black cotton. *Men!*

Well, if nothing else, the memory of this would keep her ardor toward Jeff cooled for a *loooooong* time. In the meantime, she intended to nip this disgusting habit in the bud.

"Oh, Jeff," she called out in a deceptively sweet tone. "Would you come down here for a minute?"

A muffled "just a sec" reverberated from the ceiling above her, and then she heard the *thud-thud-thud* of his footsteps on the wooden stairs.

When his face appeared, she held up another of his sock balls. "Do you think in the future you could pull these out so I don't have to stick my hand in this sweaty mess when I do the laundry?"

He cocked his head and offered a wintry smile. "Who told you to wash my clothes?"

"No one," she replied. "I just thought I'd do something nice."

"Well, next time you want to do something nice, warn me so I can prepare. I didn't ask you to do this right now. I didn't ask you to do it at all. I'm a big boy and can wash my own clothes."

Without offering the apology she wanted, he stomped back up

the stairs while April's eyes bored twin holes in his shoulder blades.

Jeff closed the basement door and, leaning against it, sighed. He probably should apologize for not unrolling his socks. Stubbornness held him back, though. Apologizing would be akin to an admission of guilt, an admission that he expected her to do his laundry and didn't care about her feelings. Well, sorry, sister, but nothing could be further from the truth.

He'd taken care of his own laundry for years now. Why should he expect anything different in Harmony House? Besides, taking a minute to shake out his socks before dropping them into the machine had never bothered him.

Tomorrow, no doubt, Grant and Jocelyn would put their own spin on this episode, just like they had this morning. Well, let them. He'd fight back with the truth—this was a simple misunderstanding brought on by April's own stubbornness.

Yesterday he'd enjoyed watching her whip around Harmony House like Ajax's white tornado. In his own foolish self-importance, he'd believed her sudden cleaning spree had more to do with his offer to kiss her again than any ulterior motive. All the while she scrubbed and washed, he never offered to help her, nor did he attempt to stop her. He simply stayed out of her way and let her run herself out.

Finally, sometime after ten, with a barely mumbled "Good night," she'd staggered into bed.

He knew she hadn't slept well. Her restlessness revealed itself in every rustle of the bedclothes and every annoyed sigh that carried over to his side of the room. Again, he merely assumed she reran their conversation on the porch.

He'd never expected Jocelyn and Grant to showcase her actions as proof of her theories regarding men's inability to handle household responsibilities. And like a conceited idiot, he fell face-first into her silken trap. Had he known that the talk show hosts planned to bushwhack him with April's Ms. Clean routine yesterday, he might have pitched in a little.

Surely, she didn't expect to play the same game today, making him look like a sloth while she appeared as the poor, put-upon hausfrau.

Surprise, April. You're about to gain a costar in your little sideshow.

While she used his dirty socks against him, he'd have to find his own ammunition. Unfortunately, she'd done such a terrific job of sanitizing this place yesterday, he couldn't find anything to do except make the beds. And that task paid no reward. No cameras caught his simple act of consideration in the bedroom.

When she appeared in the kitchen, though, he made sure she and the audience knew how he'd spent the last five minutes.

"I made the beds," he announced with as matter-of-fact an air as he could assume.

"Congratulations," she retorted.

He let her grumpiness slide. "What would you like for lunch today?"

"I'll just have a yogurt, thank you." Striding past him, she tossed her hair over her shoulder and opened the refrigerator door.

He knew that hair signal, had seen the same action often when Emma had gotten miffed at him. Okay, so the threat to kiss her on live television might not have been the smartest thing he'd ever uttered, but she'd had it coming.

A flush crept up the back of his neck, and he ran a hand over the area to soothe the heat. Now he sounded like a kid in the school yard. *She started it, Teach. . . .*

So what if she had? His conscience pricked him. *Part of your plan was to remain patient regardless of how she overreacted. Infinite acts of love and consideration, remember?*

Relaxing his posture, he leaned against the counter and toyed with the salt and pepper shakers. "You're not going to hold a grudge over a lousy pair of socks, are you?"

She whirled around from the refrigerator's interior. "Of course not."

"So then have lunch with me." He read the hesitation in the rapid blink of her eyes and quickly pressed his advantage. "I'll even make it—*and* clean up afterward. Come on, you must have tired yourself out with all you've done since yesterday."

One hip against the fridge door to close it, she smiled. "No, really. I appreciate the offer, but I'm not hungry."

The salt and pepper shakers clinked when his fingers pushed them together a little too quickly. If the quirk to her lips gave any indication, she toyed with him, in much the same manner as he played with the condiments.

"Still," he said. "You should take a break. I wanted to help you out, but you've done such a terrific job whipping this place into shape, there was nothing left. You're done now, aren't you?"

"The only thing I still have to do is fold the laundry when it comes out of the dryer."

Immediately, he straightened, ready to walk down to the basement. "I'll get that. You just sit and enjoy your yogurt."

"You might want to wait until the washing machine finishes its cycle," she called after him in a singsong voice.

In the middle of the hallway, his hand on the knob to the basement door, he stopped. A familiar heat infused him from shoulders to neck. In his eagerness to gain one up on her, he'd made himself look like an idiot.

"Actually, I was heading toward the bathroom," he said, switching direction slightly.

From her dubious expression, he realized she didn't buy that excuse any more than she'd buy the Brooklyn Bridge. To her credit, though, she didn't call him on the lie in front of the cameras. She simply twisted her lips in a doubtful smile, then returned her gaze to the plastic cup of strawberry yogurt on the counter. Strengthening the falsehood, Jeff walked down the hallway and entered the bathroom.

April heard the door click and shook her head. He must think her stupid. He was tripping over himself to help her all of a sudden, and she was supposed to think he was concerned about her, like Grant and Jocelyn's little ambush earlier had nothing to do with his change of heart.

Thinking of the interview this morning reminded her she still needed to come up with a defense plan to keep his mouth off hers. Housecleaning would only go so far. Finished with the last spoonful of yogurt, she tossed the cup into the garbage beside her, and then reached into a drawer for a pad and a pen.

She stared at the blank pad for what seemed like hours, willing words to appear, but nothing came to her. Finally, she gave up. Jeff couldn't surprise her with his kiss threat again, anyway. Besides, she normally worked better without a safety net. For now, she decided to focus her excess energy on more important things.

The pen automatically flowed over the words *Dear Michael, I sure miss you. Are you having a good time with Dad?*

"Plotting strategies?" Jeff's husky voice was low in her ear.

"Holy cow!" She nearly toppled off the stool at his sudden question. "Do you mind not sneaking up on me?" Glowering at him, she ran a hand over her nape to soothe the prickly hairs he'd triggered.

"I didn't sneak up on you. You were so enthralled with whatever you've got there you never heard me. What are you writing? Secret plans to make me look bad so you can win the challenge?"

She laughed to hide her discomfort. He came too close to the truth with that one. "Nothing so devious, I'm afraid. Just a letter to my son. After that, I'll write one for my daughter."

The stool beside her squealed as he dragged it closer, then plopped himself atop it. "You know we don't get mail delivery here."

"I know. But I thought if I can convince David they don't contain any contraband, he might mail them for me. If not, then I'll just save them until I'm released from Harmony House Prison. At least my kids will know I was thinking about them while I served my time."

He leaned an elbow on the counter and rested his chin on his hand. Instinctively, April leaned closer to her letter, hiding the words from him. If he noticed, he didn't react.

"You must miss your kids a lot."

Wow, are you barking up the wrong tree, pal! You will not use my kids as a weapon against me.

"You have no idea."

To her surprise, he dropped the subject. "How about we pull out one of those board games?"

Oh, sure, so you can pull your wine trick again?

"Not right now, thanks."

He paced the kitchen behind her until the constant back and forth sent an army of annoyance marching down her spine. When the pacing continued for nearly thirty minutes, she considered tying him to a chair.

Just when she decided to retrieve the excess clothesline, he popped his head across her writing pad. "I think I'll make tuna salad for lunch."

"I'm very happy for you."

"Would you like some?"

"No, thank you."

"Okay, then." He straightened and walked to the pantry.

Relieved at having him occupied with some task, however lame, April returned her attention to her letter. *I don't know if you've seen any of the television footage (unless Dad or Lori taped it for you), because you should be in school, but so far, I'm holding my own against—*

"Oh, for God's sake, where is the blasted tuna?" Jeff's noisy fumbling in the pantry broke her concentration. "You'd think with a cabinet this deep, someone would have thought to mount a light inside."

Slamming her palm on the counter, she rose from her stool, abandoning her letter for a quieter time and place—maybe a foxhole in Afghanistan.

"Move," she ordered, emphasizing her demand with a quick nudge of her elbow to his chest. A split second later, she held the can before his face. "Right here in the front, Jeff."

"Well, I probably moved it into the line of sight while I was digging in the back," he mumbled.

"Uh-huh."

Men. She'd never come across *one* who could find an item in a pantry, a closet, or a garage unless it sprouted arms and waved with wild abandon.

While she watched him, her impatience growing, he spun around the kitchen, that puzzled look never leaving his face. "Where's the can opener?"

Exhaling with a sigh, she opened the utensil drawer and pulled out the necessary item.

"What's that?" he asked, turning the can opener over in his hands as if it were an ancient relic from an archaeological dig.

"A can opener, silly!"

"Don't we have an electric one?"

She shook her head. "'Fraid not."

"Well, then, how do you use one of these things?"

Lips twisted in a smirk, she took the opener and can from him. "Here." She clamped the jaws of the opener around the can's rim and cranked the handle a few times. "Just like this. You think you can take it from here, *Doctor*?"

"No need to get snotty," he replied. "I've just never seen one of these before." He took the can from her. "Thank you. I'm sure I'll be fine now. Go on back to your letter."

April knew better than to even try. She returned to her seat and waited patiently, counting to herself.

One . . . two . . . three . . . four . . . five—

"Oh, for goodness sake!"

She'd reached five before the next catastrophe struck. Not bad. "What do you need now?"

"I spilled tuna juice all over myself trying to take the lid off."

Not only had he gotten the fishy liquid on himself, he'd spilled smelly droplets all over the floor—the floor she'd scrubbed clean yesterday.

"Okay, Jeff, you win." With another exasperated head shake, she grabbed a roll of paper towels and knelt to wipe up the mess. "Go change your clothes before you have every cat for miles howling outside our door. Then you can start a fire for us while I make your lunch."

"Oh, no, you don't. You just want to make me look inept in the kitchen."

"You're doing a fairly good job of that on your own," she replied. "Now go."

Chapter Eighteen

In the morning, circles deeper than the Grand Canyon ringed April's swollen eyes. Another restless night had done little for her complexion. From the other side of the bedroom, Jeff had heard her every toss and turn but could come up with no viable solution besides knocking her unconscious with a brick. And since bricks were scarce in their little wooden cabin . . .

Still, a twinge of guilt prodded his conscience at seeing her pale cheeks and gaunt face, particularly in the harsh lighting the production crew insisted on setting up over their heads. Maybe he'd take it easy on her today, let her win an argument for once. With a full weekend staring him in the eyes, he really hoped they could come to some truce to make the next two days bearable.

He changed his mind quickly, though. As if her appearance garnered sympathy for her, the producers of *Taking Sides* opened with what Jeff now termed the Sock Debacle.

"So, Dr. Jeff," Jocelyn chimed in after they aired the argument in the basement, "will you pull your socks out when you take them off from now on?"

"Since I'm accustomed to doing my own laundry," he replied, "it never occurred to me that someone else might find that little chore disagreeable."

"Disgusting is more like it," April grumbled.

"Uh-oh." Grant chuckled. "Looks like you've forgotten the rules in your own book, Dr. Jeff. A considerate man wouldn't have left his socks in a sweaty ball in a hamper. Don't you think so, ladies and gentlemen?"

The audience's claps and cheers sounded like chattering

119

monkeys in Jeff's earpiece. So much for letting her win one. He couldn't if Grant and Jocelyn planned to make him the bad guy in this scenario.

Fuming inside, he forced a lighthearted air. "I think you're making too much of an innocent mistake. Such an error on my part merely reflects the pitfalls of forcing two people who are virtual strangers to live together. There's bound to be a getting-to-know-each-other period, a time where we discover individual idiosyncrasies, pet peeves, and the like. We need time to determine what our boundaries are. Then we'll build from there."

"Sounds like backpedaling to me," Grant replied. "What do you think, April?"

"Oh, I definitely agree with you, Grant." On the couch beside Jeff, a suddenly animated April rose to tuck her feet beneath her haunches. Her new cheerfulness irked him more than Grant's schoolboy taunting. "Because it isn't only the socks that have come between us in the last five days. There's the whiskers in the bathroom sink each morning, the unrinsed dishes with food hardening in the kitchen after dinner each night, and his aversion to replacing a toilet paper roll when there's nothing left but the cardboard tube. Maybe Dr. Jeff has lived the life of a bachelor too long. Or perhaps he doesn't remember Chapter Three of *Love Is a Contact Sport,* where he talks about simple considerations going a long way."

The audience's *"ooh"* smacked him with the force of a cold ocean wave, and steam rose from his shoulders and neck. Where did all that animosity come from? For five days, she'd never mentioned his whiskers in the sink or rinsing the dishes after a meal. What a sneaky way to get her point across!

Deep inside, however, a small voice of reason called to him, reminded him he should get his emotions under control or he'd never win the audience back to his side of the argument.

"I haven't forgotten," he said through a tight smile, "but I was relying more on Chapter Eight: Respecting Personal Space. Perhaps you didn't get that far in your reading, April?"

She winced at his zinger, but the fury brewing in her eyes signaled a tiny victory for his side. Only self-control kept him from licking a finger and raising it to an invisible chalkboard.

"Actually, I have," she replied. She'd stopped bouncing on the couch now and returned to a more sedate seated position. "Though I can't begin to imagine what 'personal space' might have to do with my doing the laundry or the other activities I stated."

"It's really quite simple. As I've already mentioned, I never expected you to do my laundry. You did not inform me you planned to do my laundry. Therefore, your rummaging through my hamper could be considered an invasion of my privacy."

"I thought you'd appreciate my kindness!"

"Do you appreciate being chastised when someone does you a favor? If someone washes your car, does that give him the right to complain that it was dirty to begin with?"

"I wasn't chastising you. I merely wanted you to be aware of how revolting a habit like not pulling your socks out could be to the person stuck doing your laundry."

Ah, she'd stepped in her own mess now. It was time to go in for the kill.

"Stuck? Who said you were 'stuck' doing anything? You took it upon yourself to assume the role of laundress. No one assigned the task to you. As to the other flaws you mentioned, all you had to do was ask and I would have taken care of them myself. In case you haven't noticed, the drain in the bathroom sink is very slow. If I waited until the water flowed out and then rinsed the basin, you wouldn't have time for your shower before the production crew shows up each morning." He turned slightly in his seat, facing her florid complexion head-on. "A simple solution would have been to mention your problems to me before airing them to a national audience. Then we might have come to some reasonable compromise, like you rising a little earlier in the morning to avoid a last-minute rush. Perhaps you should strengthen your communication skills to avoid future misunderstandings between us."

Color faded from her cheeks, leaving them chalk white. "Touché, Dr. Jeff," she whispered. "You're absolutely right. From now on, I'll be sure to discuss my disagreements with you before I act to improve them."

That quickly, she'd turned the audience to her side. He heard the incriminating silence that filled his earpiece. He pictured a frown on every face filling the studio—from that of the ancient lady who showed up twice a month to that of the janitor who waxed the floor after each taping. They all thought he'd bullied her into admitting defeat when the episode should have showcased the usual lively debate. If it hadn't been for the camera staring him in the face, he would have squirmed. As it was, he could do nothing but sit stoically and wait for the torture to end.

Thanks to Jocelyn's chatterbox nature, he didn't have to wait long.

"And yet, Dr. Jeff, you couldn't make your lunch yesterday without April's help. Ladies and gentlemen, take a look at what occurred a mere thirty minutes after April left the laundry in the basement."

Amid chuckles and guffaws rattling his earphone, his comedy of errors with the can opener played out for all to see. So they weren't through ganging up on him, were they? He should have known. These two were the rabid dogs of daytime television. They never let anyone off the hook, even a regular guest who had a professional relationship with them.

"It seems to me that April has proven her point admirably today," Grant said. "Thanks to both of you for giving us so much to mull over this week. Have a great weekend, Dr. Jeff, April, and we'll speak to you again on Monday."

The red light on the camera before them went dark. That was the end of the segment? Wouldn't they give him another opportunity to respond?

"Great work, guys!" David announced, clapping. "This has been a terrific week. You two are more perfect together than I could have ever dreamed."

While the production team packed up, April rose from the couch and headed toward the hallway.

"Just a sec, April," David called out, stopping her in her tracks.

She turned, her arms folded over her chest and a frown marring her features. "What is it now? Isn't this circus closed for two days?"

"Yes, but I want to make sure you don't disappear on me. I'll be back around four o'clock this afternoon with a surprise for you guys."

"Thanks, but I'll pass. I've had enough surprises to last a lifetime."

"Trust me, sweetie, this is one you won't want to miss."

"Well, you know where to find me." Her eyes became glacial as she spread her arms wide. "Where could I possibly go? But call me sweetie again and the police'll be using dogs to sniff out your remains in the woods. Got it?"

She turned again, stalked the rest of the way down the hall, and closed the bedroom door.

David watched her for a moment, chuckled, then poked Jeff in the ribs. "Good luck with your Viking wench, Doc. I'll see you this afternoon."

April sank into the bed and stared up at the skylight, seeing nothing. Through a haze of resentment, she heard David say goodbye, heard the roar of his Jaguar outside and the spitting gravel as he sped out of the driveway and onto the road. Good riddance to the weasel.

Once again, she and Jeff were alone, this time for two whole days, with nothing but David's afternoon "surprise" to break the monotony. An insane wish to burrow under the covers until the end of the month overwhelmed her, and she had to clamp her feet to the mattress to keep from surrendering. Still, she couldn't face Jeff right now either.

During their on-air debate today, Jeff had already drawn blood once. She'd die before she gave him another opportunity to wound her. Sighing, she focused her gaze on the view above her head. Lemony sunlight, pale and bitter, met her gaze, providing no real warmth and little illumination. She tossed an imaginary rock at the glass. Five days. Only five days had elapsed since this torture began.

Time may fly when you're having fun, but when you're miserable, time's in gridlock.

Inertia set in, weighing down her limbs, sinking her deeper and deeper into the mattress. She couldn't get up if she tried—not that she wanted to. Rerunning today's disaster with Dr. Jeff kept her pinned beneath a mire of self-loathing. Unfortunately, she couldn't direct that anger onto anyone but herself. This whole mess was her fault: for jumping into this idiocy to begin with, for thinking she could hold her own against a guy with a PhD and an ego the size of Wyoming, for being born in the first place . . .

Bitterness filled April's throat.

Note to self: Never bluff an author on his own work.

It was great advice, but too late. Why? Why had she pulled the tiger's tail with no weapon more effective than a milk stool? Didn't most wild animal trainers have a whip too? Not April. Apparently, she liked to live on the edge.

One of her mother's favorite rebukes played like a broken record: *Oh, April. Why do you always think you can bluff your way through real life?*

Because I'm not good at real life, Mom. I never have been. You always told me I live by the seat of my pants. Why should this scenario be any different?

Nothing ever went smoothly for April. Okay, so lying here in her fortress of self-pity, running all the shoulda-woulda-couldas through her head, wouldn't solve anything. The time had come to force the doldrums back into their little closet in the farthest corner of her brain.

Despite today's episode, which bent more toward her side of the debate, she felt the audience's strong attraction to Jeff and, by association, his argument about infinite acts of love and consideration. Who could blame them, really? The man had a charm a rabid wildebeest couldn't ignore. And she might have been called a lot of things in her time, but a rabid wildebeest wasn't one of them. That didn't mean, however, she intended to become another of his adoring fans.

God, she hated this! She hated what she'd become—a woman looking for ulterior motives around every gesture while hiding her own ulterior motives at the same time. What would Bette Davis say about this situation? April doubted her idol would be proud.

A tentative knock stopped her pursuit of that train of thought. "April?" Jeff's hesitant question penetrated her inner sanctum. "You okay?"

"Just peachy," she sang back with forced whimsy.

Only extreme effort compelled her to sit up and place her feet on the floor.

April, my gal, get a grip. A whole weekend is staring you in the face with nothing but Jeff's company to break up the monotony. Therefore, it would behoove you to get along with the guy, no matter how much he rankles sometimes. . . .

Once on her feet, she managed to walk to the door and open it, a carefree smile pasted on her face. He'd never know how much energy she expended to feign nonchalance. "What's up?"

He quirked an eyebrow at her and folded his arms over his chest. "I was about to ask you the same thing."

"Really? Why?"

"Your threatening David comes to mind."

She waved him off. "That boy has a tendency to rub me the wrong way. I'll apologize to him when he comes back later." Which reminded her . . . "Did he happen to tell you what the surprise was?"

"Nope. Any guesses?"

She shrugged. "You know him better than I do."

"I really don't. Every time I think I've seen the worst of him, he manages to lower my opinion another notch."

"That's what scares me." Shivers rippled up her flesh, and she hugged her arms to bring them under control. "He's a real weasel, isn't he?"

"Most television producers are. I think they all have some rodent DNA in their genes. Why else would they go into this line of work? So . . ." He clapped his hands. "What should we do until four o'clock? Any thoughts or preferences?"

"None. But I'm going stir-crazy stuck in this house."

"We could go for a hike in the woods." His gaze scanned her

soft pink sweater and sparkly jeans. "I don't suppose you packed hiking boots."

"I don't even own hiking boots."

He grinned, and his smile hit her in the backs of the knees. "To be honest, neither do I."

Her fingernails dug into the molding around the doorjamb, sending painful reinforcements to her jellied legs. "I think . . . I need some fresh air."

"Good idea," he replied, and clasped her wrist. "We could probably both use a change of scenery. Come on. Let's go for a walk."

Chapter Nineteen

With her mind still focused on all that had gone wrong in her life, April followed Jeff out of the cabin. At least he didn't press her into talking. Thank goodness. She couldn't bear another therapy session today.

Frigid mountain air, tinged with the dry smell of autumn, ripped through her polyester jacket and sent goose bumps across her flesh. She shivered. Her breath left her mouth in erratic puffs of smoke.

"You should have brought your winter coat up here instead of that flimsy thing," Jeff said.

"This *is* my winter coat."

She expected him to say something about that, something about her lack of common sense or her stubborn nature. God knew her mother would.

Jeff, however, looked at her curiously for a long moment but didn't say a word. She shivered again, this time as a result of his scrutiny. He probably had a different coat in his closet for every condition imaginable—even locusts. Not her. She had one coat for all seasons.

"Do you want to go back to the house?" he finally asked.

Not on your life. The last thing she wanted was to go back into that A-frame prison cell when freedom tasted so sweet. She shook her head, fighting off another round of shivers. "I-I'll b-be . . . ," she managed to say through chattering teeth, "f-fine."

He laughed. "Come here, silly." Without waiting for a reply, he pulled her up against him, wrapping his arm around her shoulders.

She probably should have balked, should have come up with a

cutting Bette Davis–style remark and stepped away from him, but with Jeff's body as a buffer, the cold had become less brutal. It would be stupid to walk around shivering when she had a perfectly good shield from the weather, willing and able to protect her. Susan and Alan Raine's eldest daughter might be stubborn, but she wasn't stupid.

They walked a while in this manner, awkward at first but they soon found an easy rhythm of left foot, right foot, left foot, right foot. April stifled a snicker as she recalled her son's Dr. Seuss book with that very rhythm. *Always trust the classics. . . .*

Dry maple leaves blew across her feet, and soft pine needles cushioned every step. Skeletal tree limbs reached bony fingers toward a pewter sky. Yet as cold and morose as the setting was, April reveled in the atmosphere. She saw no walls, no roof, and, best of all, no cameras. *Ah, peace.*

To her right, a squirrel skittered down a tree trunk, crackling the silence. Its tail twitched as it paused, looked at the two intruders with something akin to curiosity, then bounded over a fallen log and disappeared. *Lucky squirrel.* She sighed in envy.

"You okay?" Jeff asked her.

"Uh-huh."

No other words passed between them. The farther they walked, the more April's spirit renewed itself. So she had made a series of missteps today. So what? She'd regain her lost ground by sometime next week. She'd see to it.

Resolute again, she inched out from under Jeff's arm. A blur of motion in a nearby copse caught her eye, and she slipped forward. A doe and fawn tentatively made their way across a narrow stream about twenty yards ahead. As if hearing April approach, the fawn looked up, its soulful, slanted eyes connecting directly with April's heart.

Michael. The fawn's eyes reminded her of her son's eyes, of that special upward slant, caused by an epicanthal fold, which made him unique. God, she missed the sight of those wondrous eyes—eyes that saw the world as new and exciting every single day. She should be home with him, not here with a stranger. The hammer of guilt nearly drove her to her knees.

"April?" Jeff's husky voice reached her through a cacophony of remorse.

"I . . . think . . . ," she murmured, her focus still on the baby deer, "I want to go back now."

For two and a half hours, Jeff did everything he could think of to get April out of whatever funk she'd spun for herself—to no avail. She wouldn't eat, wouldn't speak at all; she simply moped, sighed, and paced until he grew depressed just watching her.

If he'd known she'd get this morose because she had lost an argument, he might have let her win, because now he faced the prospect of an entire weekend with stormy April Raine. What on earth had he said to bring this on? Or had he said anything at all?

With a sense of doom, he remembered Emma's frenetic mood swings, particularly toward the end. Happy one minute, raging the next.

No, he told himself firmly. April had no such problems. Whatever caused her change in behavior now had nothing to do with artificial stimuli. He'd bet his license on that. She was quiet, yes, but not in any dangerous way that he could see.

Besides, a woman like April, so different from Emma on a thousand levels, would never be seduced by the promises found in starving herself into oblivion. From what he knew of her, he didn't think that April could be seduced by promises of any kind. He admired that quiet strength in her. It was one of many of April's qualities he admired.

The farsighted fool who'd lived with Emma all those years ago had disappeared. Surviving that had hardened him, made him more cynical and suspicious. So if April hid any dangerous vice at all, he would have discovered the flaw by now.

She's practically perfect.

That single thought depressed him even more than her silent pouting. It meant nothing yet everything at the same time.

If it hadn't been for David's return, Jeff would have spent the rest of the day in the same black mood as April.

"You two ready for your surprise?" David announced from the front door.

"As ready as we'll ever be," April replied flatly.

David held up a battered black telephone—an old sixties model with a dial face. "Ta-da! You'll each be allowed to make one phone call, ten minutes in duration, to anyone you wish."

April's face lit up like an airport runway at midnight. "I can call my son?"

David shrugged. "If you think he's around, sure." He placed the phone on an end table and peered over the back of the couch. "Once I find the phone jack, you can. Ah, there it is." Pulling the phone line with him, he shoved his arm between the couch and the wall. "There you are. Who wants to go first?"

As if Jeff could compete with the elation on April's face. With a quick sweep of his hand, he gestured for her to take the honors.

"Thank you," she gushed, reaching for the receiver eagerly. Her nimble fingers dialed a number that was no doubt second nature to her. A heavy silence filled the air around them, and then hope flourished in her voice. "Lori? Hi. It's April. I hope this doesn't sound rude, but I only have ten minutes. Can I talk to Michael, please?" Pause. "Becky's there too? Ohmigod, timing's everything. Put Becky on first."

An unfamiliar ache, the ache of envy, filled Jeff as he watched her bounce up and down while she waited for her daughter to come on the line.

"Becky? It's Mom. How are you doing? I miss you so much. I know. I can't believe it. Of all weekends for you to decide to spend time with your father . . ."

Jeff turned his back to give her a little privacy, the ache growing to monstrous proportions.

"How's school?"

Another pause.

"That's great. I knew you'd ace that test. Did Dad take you out to celebrate?"

Another pause.

"Shattered Glass? Isn't that the band you wanted to see in the nightclub in the city?" Her voice lost a little enthusiasm. Now disapproval crept in. "Becky, you know I didn't want you going there—"

She began to pace the floor. "Sweetheart, I only have ten minutes right now, and I really didn't want to spend that time chastising you. But I'm pretty upset about this."

The pacing became rapid. "'Why'? You know perfectly well why. We discussed that concert. You knew I didn't want you going there." She sighed. "I know you're in college, but I still don't think, at your age, you're equipped—"

Her voice lowered to a whisper. "Look, we'll talk about this when I get home."

While listening to whatever her daughter said in reply, she sank onto the couch. "I'm so proud of you. You know, I doubt I could have aced a physics test, but you did it easily. And when I get home, we'll have another celebration, okay? Just the three of us. I love you, Becky." There was a pause during which Jeff guessed Becky reciprocated her mother's affection. Then April added, "Can I talk to Michael now?"

David strode forward, intent on passing Jeff. With one hand outstretched, Jeff stopped the executive producer in mid-stride. "Where are you going?"

David pointed to his watch. "Her time's up."

"Give her my ten minutes," Jeff ordered in a hushed voice. "Let her talk to her son."

"You sure?"

Jeff glanced at April. The joy sparkling in her eyes illuminated the dim room like an angel's halo. Folding his arms over his chest, he barred the way, almost defying David to take a step toward where April sat. "No one's waiting to hear from me. Give her my time."

"Michael?" April's tone grew childlike. "How are you, baby? It's Mommy. Oh, I miss you so much!"

Against his better judgment, Jeff listened to her conversation with curiosity.

How old was her son? Twelve, if he remembered correctly. So why did she insist on talking to him in such a juvenile manner?

With Becky, she'd maintained some semblance of an adult—her normal rapid speech pattern, use of two- and three-syllable words, a focus on responsibility and grades. With Michael, she enunciated each syllable as if talking to a toddler. Her speech pattern was slower, with simpler word choices. There was no emphasis on grades or chores in her conversation with him.

Jeff got the feeling Michael was some sort of royal prince, catered to and adored. Talk about Mama's little boy . . .

For the first time since he'd met her, Jeff lost respect for this lady. After all, someone so sensitive about her parents' playing favorites among their children should take more care to avoid making the same mistake with her own kids.

Did Becky see herself as the second generation of Nobody's Darling? Would April appreciate his pointing out the possibility to her? Would any parent?

A short while later, David barreled past him. "Time's up, April."

Brow furrowed in confusion, she looked up. Then, as if remembering where she was and why, she smoothed her face. "Oh, right. Sorry." She turned her back to whisper into the phone, "I love you, baby, and I'll see you soon. I promise. Bye-bye." She replaced the receiver on its cradle and turned to face Jeff. "Your turn."

"No, April, that's it," David said, and reached to unplug the phone from the jack. "You used up all twenty minutes."

Eyes wide with dismay, April stared at Jeff. "I'm so sorry. I didn't realize—"

He waved off her apology. "It's all right. I told David to let you take my ten minutes. It's not like I have kids waiting to hear from me."

The words came out gruffer than he wanted, but if April noticed, she didn't mention it. Instead, she walked toward him, stood on tiptoe, and kissed his cheek.

"Thank you. You have no idea what that means to me."

Chapter Twenty

Saturday morning passed with little fanfare. They shared the household chores, remaining on their best behavior around the cameras. In the afternoon, they took a long walk in the woods. The fawn didn't reappear, much to April's relief, and she relaxed her guard around Jeff, blissful after his magnanimous gesture with the phone.

Oddly enough, while they walked, she talked about her marriage: about the hard times, the fun times, the many betrayals. Once she began, she couldn't stop the torrent of words. She bared every ugly layer of scar tissue while he listened. He interrupted only to comment or ask a pertinent question.

"I'm not sure I ever really loved Peter," she summed up. "I was more in love with the *idea* of Peter than the actual man."

Two brows rose—Jeff's communication of utter confusion. April bit back a smile. How strange it was that she knew all his facial expressions by now and could figure out when he was amused, interested, dubious, curious, or, as in this case, bewildered.

"You'll have to explain that," he said.

Yeah, she'd figured as much. "Peter and I were children when we met, children when we married. So it's no wonder I always had this childish vision in my head about the way our marriage was supposed to be."

"What kind of vision?"

She stopped walking, and he stopped as well. With a stern expression, she wagged a finger up at his face. "Promise not to laugh."

Hand upraised, he held his thumb across his palm. "Scout's honor."

133

"Well, if you must know . . . in the early years of our marriage, I spent a lot of time fantasizing about all the family sitcoms I grew up watching. Of them all, I thought we would be like—"

"Don't tell me," he interrupted. "You didn't compare yourself to *The Brady Bunch,* did you?"

"Of course not. I always wanted to be like the Stephenses on *Bewitched.*"

A snicker escaped his lips, and she whirled on him. "You promised. Remember? 'Scout's honor'?"

"Yes, but I was never a Scout."

She stamped a foot in indignation. "You know, you really stink."

He laughed so loud several crows, seated on branches above them, squawked their displeasure at the noise before flapping off in a huff.

"I'm sorry," he said through chuckles, "but the idea of you as Samantha Stephens, twitching your nose . . ."

Heat filled her face, and she hurried to defend her naïveté. "I wasn't talking about being able to perform magic, for God's sake. Besides, I was just a kid. How old were you when you met your wife?"

"Twenty-five."

"So you had ten years on me. Ten important, maturing years. And I bet there were still things about your wife you only discovered after you married her. Like that not-being-able-to-cook thing you told me about. So when I married Peter, I was expecting him to be like Darrin Stephens."

"You thought a new actor would step in to play the role after the first few years?"

"You're not taking me seriously at all." Her fists stuffed in her pockets, she strode away from him.

She got a few feet ahead before his arm encircled her waist and pulled her against his chest.

"Okay, okay. I'm sorry."

She liked the way he felt wrapped around her, at once protective and dangerous. It was exciting, in an odd kind of way. Confused about what that might mean, she forced herself to remember their conversation. Feigning a grudge, she tilted her chin up and pulled out of his grasp. "Nope. Forget it. I'm not talking to you anymore."

"I'm sorry. Honest. You were saying?"

"Forget it," she repeated. "You hurt my feelings."

"Aw, c'mon. What can I do to make it up to you?"

That was a question more loaded than an AK-47. For now, she ignored the invitation and concentrated on keeping her face safe from spontaneous combustion.

"Fine." She heaved a tremendous sigh, as if her capitulation came at great cost. "I know it sounds stupid, but I thought that Peter would work hard enough to take care of his family. I counted on it, as a matter of fact. Depended on it."

" 'Independence is the greatest gift we're given in life.' "

He remembered that? The realization brought a sparkle of delight to her insides. She touched her index finger to her nose. "Exactly. I bet my independence on the wrong horse."

"I think he had more to do with that problem than you did."

"No, it was my fault. I never saw the real Peter, always too enthralled with the Peter–slash–Darrin Stephens of my dreams. He couldn't compete with my fantasy." Sighing at the bitter memories, she leaned against a tree trunk. "And apparently, I couldn't compete with his."

"Did you know he was cheating on you?"

The question, spoken tentatively, still stung, and she retorted without thinking. "I might have been a naïve kid, but I wasn't stupid. Or blind."

"So why did you put up with it?"

"Not because I was in love with him, if that's what you're thinking. And I did throw him out eventually."

She remembered every emotion she'd experienced. The anger, betrayal, and shame. How she'd fume every time she found a strange phone number in Peter's pocket or smelled an unusual fragrance on his shirt collar. The nights of wondering who, when, and where. The dread she'd run into a neighbor at the grocery story or the Laundromat who'd smile sympathetically while secretly laughing at her naïveté. And the effort to paste a smile on her face for the kids, praying they'd never find out. And all the while, she'd considered the multitude of methods she wanted to employ to neuter her husband.

When her mind could no longer rise above the flood of emotions on a regular basis, she took action. One sunny Tuesday, she headed for their shared closet. Every item he owned, wore, or ever touched found its way into an open suitcase. Dirty, clean, it didn't matter. His rank sweat mixed with the chemicals he used in his business and formed a pungent odor. Secretly, she hoped the foul smell would seep into all his garments and stay there forever, a perfect scarlet letter for him to wear in public.

Once the suitcase was filled to the brim, she sat on the lid to lock it, carried it to the front door, and waited for Peter to come home so she could confront him with all the rage brewing in her veins. But the joke was on her. Peter didn't come home that night. He called to say he was working late and waited until the next morning to appear.

Before she could accuse him of anything, though, he told her he planned to leave her for the company's secretary, thanked her for packing his things, and walked out. The minute the door closed behind him, she headed for the phone in the kitchen. She found a lawyer in the Yellow Pages—not a terrific site for a referral, and that was when *desperation* became her mother of invention.

Luckily, the lawyer her fingers found was capable and honest. An hour after meeting with April, Judith Polhemus, Esquire, started divorce proceedings and worked to gain April full custody of her children.

A thrill of triumph elated April a few weeks later when she heard from Judith that Peter had broken up with the secretary. But the thrill didn't last long. He'd ditched the secretary for Lori. Well, Peter had become *her* problem now.

"Why didn't you leave him after the first time?" Jeff's question brought her back to the present with a jolt. "Or the second or third? Why did you put up with his cheating for so long?" Her brewing anger must have registered on her face, because he held up a hand. "I'm not trying to insult you. I've just always been curious about why women stay in that kind of situation."

She shrugged. "Well, I can't speak for all women, but I stayed because I blamed myself for his weakness. I thought it was my fault he felt the need to cheat. I assumed I must have been doing something wrong: I wasn't attractive enough, smart enough, or exciting enough to keep his attention. If I hadn't been lacking in some way, he wouldn't have looked elsewhere." She gave a bitter smile. "I know what you're thinking. Nobody's Darling strikes again, right?"

He shook his head, but she didn't believe him.

Didn't all shrinks connect adult problems with those from childhood? Since Mommy and Daddy didn't find her perfect the way she was, any psychologist would make the leap that her marriage suffered from the same issues.

"So what changed your mind?"

She kicked at an errant pebble in the dirt, secretly wishing it was Peter's heart. "I just woke up one day and I realized his destructive behavior—because, let's face it, that's what it was—was due to something inside of him, not me. Even if I'd made myself into his dream woman and locked him in our bedroom twenty-four seven, he still would have found a way to get out and chase other women. It was his weakness, not mine. Probably still is. And he won't stop until he's ready or until he's dead, whichever comes first. No amount of love or effort on my part can change what's inherent in his nature."

After dinner, Jeff stared into the flames in the fireplace while April took a bath. Although he sat on a comfortable chair inside the warm cabin, his mind remained in the cold woods, listening to April discuss her marriage.

It was his weakness, not mine. Probably still is. And he won't stop until he's ready or until he's dead, whichever comes first.

Once again, April had managed to shake up his perceptions of Emma—this time for the worse. Even if her comments struck their mark indirectly, she'd hit a perfect bull's-eye. With all the platitudes and expressions of sympathy he'd heard over the years, no one had ever broken the tragedy down to its lowest common denominator. But April had, without even realizing it.

No amount of love or effort on my part can change what's inherent in his nature.

Brilliant. She constantly amazed him.

A scientist by nature, Jeff didn't believe in fate. Yet the professor's words from long ago echoed inside his brain. *No one comes into your life without a purpose. Each person you meet, no matter how briefly, is sent to teach you or be taught by you.*

He'd assumed he'd teach April a thing or two over these thirty days. Yet meeting and living with April had opened his eyes in a way no scientific method could. She'd taught him a great deal about himself and, more important, about Emma.

She's a better psychologist than I am.

"Well?"

The subject of his musings stood in the hallway, her hair wrapped turban-style and a thick terry cloth robe nearly swallowing her tiny frame.

Shoot. While she took a bath, he was supposed to load the dishwasher. Instead, he'd sunk into the nearest chair to brood. Either she'd opted for a sponge bath or he'd lost track of time. Since April looked relaxed and thoroughly languid, he was to blame for the dirty dishes still on the table.

He'd have to do some serious backpedaling on the issue or look like a fool for the television cameras.

"How do women manage to do that with a towel?" he asked, pointing to the turban.

She smirked. "It's one of those female tricks we discuss when men aren't around. I could tell you, but then I'd have to kill you." Her gaze flicked to the messy table and she frowned. "You didn't clear the table yet? Is something wrong?"

He smoothed his brow and leaned back in the chair, the picture of relaxation. "No, of course not. I got distracted is all."

"Uh-huh." She stared at the empty furniture, the barren walls. "By what?"

"Nothing important."

She folded her arms over her chest. "Yet it was important enough for you to forget about the dishes."

Her posture took on the look of a scolding mama, and resentment boiled up from his gut. "Lots of things in life are more important than a bunch of dirty dishes," he said, his voice growing chillier with each syllable. "That doesn't mean I need to pour my heart and soul out to you. Or anybody else, for that matter."

"Who said anything about pouring out your heart and soul? I just want to know why the dishes are still on the table."

"Because I got distracted. By what, is none of your business."

"I see," she replied, her tone icy calm. "So my life's an open book, but yours is an armored car?"

"What open book?"

"I confided in you this afternoon, but, apparently, you don't feel the need to reciprocate."

"You told me about your husband's dozens of other women outdoors, remember? *Away* from the cameras."

The minute the words left his mouth, he knew he'd screwed up big-time.

Her eyes reflected hurt and shock. "You know what? You're a real jerk."

Before he could apologize, she turned and huffed down the hall to the bedroom. Ten seconds after the door closed with a slam, a light snick said quite definitively that she'd locked him out.

Chapter Twenty-one

Sunday came and went with no truce between them. April didn't think she could ever forgive Jeff for airing her dirty laundry publicly. Rather than growl at him every time she passed, which would give the cameras extra fodder for Monday, she remained locked inside the bedroom, vacillating between rage and humiliation. Morning turned to afternoon. Afternoon turned to evening.

Jeff knocked once—to ask for his clothes. She told him he had plenty of clean stuff folded in a hamper in the basement. No way was he getting into the bedroom. Night arrived again. Still April paced ruts in the hardwood floor, reliving every word she'd spoken to Jeff and wishing for ways to turn back time.

If she'd known he would humiliate her, she wouldn't have confided in him. Heck, why not go all the way back? If she'd known what would happen in this house, she would have told off the network execs when they'd first approached her. Dr. Jeff could have put her company on his unfriendly list until doomsday. She would have found some way to combat his negative publicity. Eventually.

If only she'd kept her distance from *Taking Sides* . . . If only she hadn't agreed to this challenge . . . If only she hadn't allowed Jeff's acts of love and consideration to lower her guard . . .

Steam rose up her throat and blew out her eardrums. How dared he embarrass her that way? Jocelyn and Grant would have a field day with Jeff's comment about Peter's "dozens of other women." What kind of psychologist blabs personal information to a nationwide audience?

The quack kind, she thought. *No wonder he's the resident psychologist for* Taking Sides. *Only a soulless television show would hire such an unprofessional, uncaring, un . . . un . . . un*human *individual to heal the mentally battered. He probably took the job because no private practice would have him.*

Before long, Monday arrived. Jeff didn't bring her coffee in bed, since she'd locked him out, but she did notice he had cleaned his shaving leftovers out of the bathroom sink.

Some kind of peace offering, maybe? Didn't matter. She was still too furious to get all warm and gooey over pristine pink porcelain. After a quick shower and an even quicker wardrobe change, she slapped some makeup on her face and left the safety of the bedroom to enter the living room—or, as she'd come to think of it, the gladiators' arena.

She bypassed Jeff, already in his spot on the left of the couch, and took her place on the right.

"Good morning, gentlemen," she said to the production crew gathered around her. Her gaze traveled the semicircle of males standing just outside the arena and deliberately avoided any contact with the lone male seated closest to her. She clipped the earphone into place with practiced dexterity. "Let's get this done, shall we?"

"April," Jeff whispered through barely parted lips. "We should talk."

"Oh, we will," she promised, giving him her full attention for the first time in thirty-six hours. "As soon as Jocelyn and Grant join us."

"Look, I'm sorry about the other night—"

"Save it," she interrupted, each word icy and succinct. "You embarrassed me publicly, you can atone publicly."

"Okay." He imitated her frosty tone. "Fine. Have it your way."

Despite bands of steel cinched around her abdomen, April forced herself to appear relaxed and thoroughly in control. Bette Davis to the max. What would Bette think of all this? Probably something along the lines of "Everybody has a heart. Except some people."

One of those "some people" sat next to her now, and two more waited in a television studio in Manhattan to rake her over the coals.

The red light above the main camera blinked and then glowed steadily. They were on the air.

"Good morning, Dr. Jeff, April." Jocelyn's chipper voice bristled hackles on April's neck.

"Good morning, Jocelyn," she managed to say with some semblance of cheerfulness.

"Well, you two certainly had an eventful weekend. First you received a surprise from our executive producer. April, why don't you tell us about that?"

Relaxing her guard at the memory, April smiled. "I was allowed to phone my children."

She heard a group "awww . . ." followed by a smattering of applause.

"That must have felt great," Grant said enthusiastically.

"It did, Grant. I've never been away from them for so long before, so to hear their voices and to be able to let them know I was okay was a very big deal for me."

"That's terrific. Now, according to our executive producer, you and Dr. Jeff were each allotted ten minutes to speak with whomever you wished."

She knew where they headed with this, and guilt darted into her conscience with pinpoint accuracy. "Yes, that's true."

"But Dr. Jeff didn't use the telephone, did he? In fact, he offered you his time so that you could speak to your children for an entire twenty minutes. Isn't that right?"

"Yes, he did. And I was very grateful to him for his generosity."

"We have a clip of you showing your gratitude," Jocelyn announced. "Ladies and gentlemen, if you'll watch the monitors . . ."

April didn't have a monitor to watch, but she remembered the incident well enough. And when another emotional "awwww . . ." resounded from the crowd, she guessed they'd played the kiss she'd given Jeff's cheek.

"Jeff, why did you give up your time for April?"

"The telephone call seemed more important to her than to me.

In the short time I've known her, I've discovered how very much she loves her children. To give up my time so she could spend a few more minutes with them was a small sacrifice on my part."

"And based on April's reaction," Grant added, "your 'small sacrifice' went a long way toward proving your point about acts of consideration."

"True," Jeff replied, and crossed one leg over the other thigh.

April's fingers curled into her palms, and an overwhelming urge to punch him in the gut rose within her.

Manipulative jerk. Manipulative, blabbermouthy jerk. Make yourself look good when you know exactly what's coming next— and how it's going to decimate me.

Meanwhile, the emcees and audience ate it all up like a rich chocolate mousse.

"But," Jeff continued, "I burned the goodwill bridge later that evening."

"Would you care to discuss that, Dr. Jeff?"

"Actually," he replied, straightening on the couch, "I'd like to ask you to leave the footage regarding that particular issue un-aired. You see, April disclosed certain information to me in confidence Saturday afternoon. In a moment's distraction, I voiced that confidence aloud. It was an unforgivable breach for someone in my profession, and I'd prefer that we not compound my transgression by broadcasting what should have remained a private matter."

Mouth agape, April struggled to form a coherent thought. Her attempts probably made her resemble a beached flounder, but logic had fled. He'd turned the tables on her. Oh, he'd done exactly what she wanted him to do: apologize publicly. But in doing so, he'd managed to portray himself as the grand hero, simultaneously tossing her into the role of ungrateful schlub.

Jerk. Manipulative jerk.

From the other side of the room, David flashed a thumbs-up sign, and April's blood pressure boiled over. These two had planned the whole thing, to make her look ridiculous. Worse, they'd succeeded.

In her own indomitable way, she'd helped them—a mistake she didn't intend to make again.

When Grant and Jocelyn finally said good-bye, April didn't wait to be sure the cameras shut down before she yanked off the mike and earphone and tossed the offending articles on the couch.

"It's been real," she told the men around her, and stalked into the kitchen.

Bette Davis had certainly known what she was talking about when she'd said, "One cannot, in any shape or form, depend on human relations for lasting reward. It is only work that truly satisfies."

Work. So that was what April intended to do. In the cabinet under the sink, she found a can of oven cleaner and a pair of yellow latex gloves. Perfect. She'd focus her energies on crusty crud for starters.

She had her head and half her torso inside the wall oven when she heard Dr. Jeff's amused voice behind her. "Suicide? I thought better of you, April."

Knowing he couldn't see her in her current position, she made a screwy face as she imitated his words to the lightbulb at the back of the oven. "And I would think that a psychologist worth his degree wouldn't make fun of such a serious subject."

"I'm just trying to break the ice."

She scrubbed at a particularly deep grease stain and pictured erasing Jeff with her efforts. "Yeah, well, you're failing miserably."

"I don't understand why you're so upset. I did what you wanted. I apologized publicly."

His ignorance, feigned or otherwise, boiled her oil to the explosion point. She backed out of the oven and whirled on him, blazing enough righteous indignation to cook him on the spot.

"You have to be the most manipulative . . ." She took a step toward him. ". . . underhanded . . ." Another step. ". . . arrogant . . ." Now they were nose to nose. ". . . son of a—"

His lips cut off the rest of her invective. Anger drained from her in a flood, replaced with a longing that throbbed from her heart out. Just before she allowed the tide to carry her out to sea, the soft voice of sanity whispered in her ear. What had Peter advised? Pretend Jeff was him? Well, if Jeff were Peter at this moment, how would she react? Simple.

She allowed herself to the count of ten to enjoy the whirlwind of sensations his kiss engendered. Then, at the exact moment her mind hit that magic number, she brought her heel crashing down on his toes.

"Ow!" He pulled away from her so fast the breeze ruffled her hair. "What'd you do that for?"

"Because I'm not going to fall for your mushy-gushy tactics," she retorted.

"I wasn't attempting a mushy-gushy tactic," he said, rubbing his injured toes against the back of his opposing leg.

"No? My mistake. You were obviously so taken with my stunning good looks you couldn't help but kiss me. Your threat to keep me quiet using that very method was mere coincidence."

"I've never threatened you."

Was he insane? "Should I call David and have him rewind the tape to Thursday's episode?"

His eyes widened, then narrowed. She could only surmise he'd finally remembered that on-air remark.

Folding her arms over her chest, she jutted her chin out and declared, "If you'll excuse me, I have work to do."

She returned her attention to the oven's interior seconds before the tears broke free.

Chapter Twenty-two

The next four days passed with the speed of a slug swimming in a stream of beer—uphill. By the time Friday arrived, April had about as much energy as her imagined slug. On the upside, though, she'd managed to get through the week without giving Grant, Jocelyn, or even Jeff one scintilla of salt to inflict on her.

It wasn't that Jeff hadn't tried to get back into her good graces. He picked a bunch of wildflowers for her while out running one afternoon, kept the bathroom sink clean, and washed the dishes every night after dinner. Once he even turned down the covers of her bed and placed a heart made from aluminum foil on her pillow with a note attached that read *I.O.U. one chocolate.*

April recognized most of these as acts of consideration from the pages of *Love Is a Contact Sport.* Knowing where all these gestures came from left her with a chill no fire could thaw.

Pain sliced her heart to confetti. Did he think there was a cookie cutter used to create women? A flower here, a chocolate there, and voila! She's happy again.

Sorry, Charlie. You can't get away with one-size-fits-all penance. Regardless of what panty hose manufacturers might think, there's no such thing as "one size fits all."

By now, somebody should have taught the fine Dr. Jeff that no two women were alike: some preferred roses, while others loved daisies. Of course, April didn't care for roses or daisies, didn't like flowers at all, except in a garden. Cut or picked flowers died too quickly, their memory lost in wisps of time. Michael had taught her to appreciate the here and now but save some joy for tomorrow too.

She didn't have an affinity for chocolate on her pillow, regardless of its shape, either. What woman in her right mind found that romantic? If you forgot it was there, you wound up with melted chocolate in your hair. If you ate it, you found yourself staring at the ceiling at four in the morning, thanks to a late-night sugar high. Thanks, but no thanks.

Hey, pal, wanna make me happy? Stay out of my head, keep your psychobabble away from my personal life, and stop nosing into my business. And if you want to sweep me off my feet, admit your "acts of consideration" aren't doing squat on me.

Okay, maybe that wasn't entirely true. There was something awfully decadent about sipping coffee in bed first thing in the morning. Still, she dared not grow accustomed to such luxury— not unless she planned to kidnap Jeff and take him home with her when this was all over.

Face it, kiddo. It'd be a lot easier on your moods, not to mention your heart, to buy a programmable coffee maker.

But a programmable coffee maker couldn't make her laugh, couldn't listen to her problems, couldn't help fill the lonely hours—not the way Jeff could.

She pounded a fist into her pillow. *No.* She refused to allow him to win.

Think of Michael. Think of what one hundred thousand dollars could buy him: stability, security, a future.

All the coffee in Brazil didn't compete with Michael's needs.

April's brooding drove Jeff crazy. Entombed for years in his enforced bachelorhood, he'd forgotten how moody women could get over the slightest setback. For the last six days, he'd done everything he could think of to shake her out of her doldrums, exhausting his entire repertoire of kind and thoughtful acts—to no avail.

Jeff bet if he laid his offerings at the altar of some stone goddess, he'd gain the same blasé reaction. Still, he kept trying.

On Friday, their end-of-the-week appearance aired more silence between them than discussion.

"So . . . April," Jocelyn said after the third such breakdown in conversation. "Are you looking forward to the weekend?"

April spared a scathing glance Jeff's way before replying, "Actually, Jocelyn, I'm looking forward to nothing more than going home soon."

"You must miss your children terribly."

"I miss my children, but I miss other things too." *Like my freedom.* April bit back the retort and let silence re-permeate the house in the Adirondacks, as well as the studio in New York.

"Dr. Jeff." Grant popped into the awkwardness. "Can you think of any way to shake April out of her homesickness?"

"As I've already stated," Jeff replied, crossing one leg over the other, "April is a devoted mother."

Oh, here we go. He's donning the competent-analyst veneer.

April's hackles rose to alert status.

"I'm not surprised to hear that she's second-guessing her decision to participate in this Harmony House challenge—"

"Whoa!" She interrupted his psychobabble. "Hold up. I didn't say that."

"No?" Jeff quirked a brow at her. "My mistake, then. What exactly were you saying?"

Smarmy jerk. He'd set her up good this time. No matter what she said now, she'd look like the neglectful mother, putting her children's needs below inconsequential nonsense.

Somebody help. Anybody . . .

Apparently, her idol heard her plea, because the answer came to her in a whisper.

"It's true I've found the Harmony House experiment a real challenge," she said at last. "But as Bette Davis once said, 'The key to life is accepting challenges. Once someone stops doing this, he's dead.' By the same token, once a challenge has run its course, it's dead. I honestly believe Dr. Jeff and I have reached an impasse that cannot be breached. This experiment is truly dead. Therefore, nothing else waits but our exit."

She said a silent thank-you to Bette's ghost and could've sworn she heard the dowager actress reply, "I am *too* much!"

No one in the studio said a word. No one at Harmony House said a word. And April sat, a nonplussed Jeff beside her, while the silence bloomed again.

At long last, Grant offered a pathetic "Well, I guess that's all for this week from Harmony House. Dr. Jeff, April, thanks again for speaking with us. Have a wonderful weekend."

The light above the camera went black.

"Oh, for God's sake!" David yanked the earphones off his head and tossed them on the floor. "What was that all about, April?"

She feigned an expression of pure innocence: newborn lamb meets Snow White. "Is there a problem, David?"

His eyes narrowed to slits, and fury rolled off him in palpable waves. "Forget it. Just forget it."

Several minutes passed, again in that overbearing silence, before, finally, David turned his glower on Jeff. "It looks like we're in for a real downpour. C'mon. I'll help you bring in some more firewood before I leave. You wouldn't want to have to traipse out to the woodpile in the middle of a thunderstorm."

Uh-huh. That wasn't too obscure a non sequitur. She looked at Jeff with open curiosity, but he merely shrugged and followed David out the door.

When they approached the woodpile, David whirled, glaring at Jeff like a vulture waiting for its prey to die. "What in God's name is going on with you two?"

"What do you mean?"

"You know exactly what I mean. Last week was beautiful. Then all of a sudden the weekend comes. By Monday morning, April's sitting miles away from you on the couch, stiff as a ten-day corpse. And every word that leaves her mouth drips sarcasm."

"Well, what did you expect?" Jeff snapped. "We're virtual strangers locked together in a house with no respite. Did you think we'd fall into bed within forty-eight hours?"

David's eyes narrowed. "You two had some real heat simmering between you last week. So, yeah. I think the whole world expected to see something pretty hot between you guys by now. Instead, we're left scanning hours of April walking past you without saying a word. What'd you do to screw this up?"

"Maybe she's homesick. Maybe she's second-guessing whatever drove her to show up here in the first place. I apologized for what I said, there's nothing more that I can do."

"Look, Doc. This Harmony House bit was my idea. It falters, I lose all my credibility with the network. You're Dr. Jeff, author of the most popular self-help book in the country. I'm giving you the chance to prove that *Love Is a Contact Sport* isn't just another useless pile of tripe. Now, if I were you, I'd be thinking about all the little instances of love and consideration you wrote about to see which ones will butter up April and get her hanging on your every word."

"April's distance has nothing to do with any lack of love and consideration. It's probably the stupid cameras. Neither one of us can relax with a nationwide audience watching us from every angle."

"Okay, then, I'll tell you what," the vulture offered. "I'll turn off the cameras for the weekend. Sunday night, I'll turn them back on. That gives you more than forty-eight hours to get her to soften up. I don't care if you sweep her off her feet or threaten to push her off a cliff. I'm offering you a chance to get her under control no matter what it takes. Make the most of it. Use that charm all the blue-haired ladies in the audience seem to swoon over. But by Monday, I want to see a much more pleasant April Raine."

David's smug grin conveyed his power over the situation. Jeff mustered up every ounce of self-control to keep from knocking the cocky vulture to the ground and pummeling him.

Chapter Twenty-three

With leaden feet, Jeff followed David into the house, a pile of logs gathered in his arms. April stood in the foyer with that same curious expression brewing in her eyes.

"Well, folks," David announced as he dropped his stack near the fireplace, "I've got good news and bad news. A technical glitch has shorted out our cameras. And thanks to union rules, we won't be able to get it repaired until Sunday night. Looks like you two will have some privacy over the weekend." He then shot a final warning glance in Jeff's direction. "Use the respite well."

The door closed behind him, and dead silence permeated the room until the sound of the Jaguar's engine coming to life echoed outside. Ignoring April's questioning stare, Jeff expelled a breath.

"I don't know about you, but I could use a run," he said.

Before she could respond, he strode into the bedroom and locked the door. After a quick change of clothes, he headed out of the house and into the forest to find some peace.

But running did nothing to clear Jeff's conscience. David's innuendoes and snide hints about how to manipulate April echoed in his head with each footfall on the dirt path. Ethics, however, precluded his accepting those directions.

He blamed himself for the impasse with April. Betraying her confidence, divulging her husband's infidelities on camera, was a huge mistake. He could blame the slip on grief for Emma, which had temporarily taken control of his senses.

But he refused to continue hiding behind the loss of his family. Time to face the truth—April had somehow wormed into his psyche and turned everything he'd believed upside down. Waves of gratitude washed over him. This whole Harmony House concept was the craziest, most ludicrous . . . best thing that had ever happened to him. Thanks to April.

A soft *thud-thud-thud* from behind raised the hackles on his neck. He turned to see the subject of his musings approaching fast.

"Forget the run and talk to me," April commanded as she fell into step beside him. "What's going on with you and David?"

"I don't know what you mean."

She gripped his forearm and yanked him to a stop. "Uh-huh. Right," she replied, gasping for breath. "Look, pal. If it's something that affects me, I have a right to know."

A flush crept up his nape. She was absolutely correct.

"David pulled me aside to find out if we'd had some kind of blowout. He's concerned that we're becoming too distant from each other," he admitted.

"Yeah?" She puffed a wisp of hair out of her eyes. "What does he care?"

"He fears the ratings will plummet. I told him it was very difficult for us to relax with a nationwide audience watching our every move."

She arched an eyebrow in his direction. "So is that the sudden 'technical glitch' that popped up today?"

"Yes. He offered to turn the cameras off for the weekend so we could relax our guards a little."

Her mouth opened in a wide o of understanding. "He was counting on some kind of romantic tension because we shared a couple of kisses last week, wasn't he?"

"Yup."

"What an idiot." Her giggle sent a flurry of birds flying from the trees overhead.

"Now, if you'll excuse me, I'd like to get my heart rate accelerated again." He turned around, but her hand returned to his forearm, stopping him a second time.

"Hey, wait a minute. What are we going to do about this?"

"About what?"

That pink color he loved returned to heighten her cheeks. "Okay,

I admit I was out of line and a bit of a witch the last few days, and I'm sorry. I mean, I don't give a darn what David thinks about us." Her gaze fell to the ground, and her tone grew so low he had to lean close to hear her. "But for a while I thought we were becoming friends, and I don't want to screw that up."

He bit back a smile. "You didn't screw anything up. I'm sorry too. I shouldn't have aired Peter's infidelities on camera like that."

"So we're friends again?"

"We never stopped being friends, April."

Her relief was audible in her exhale. "Good. What happens now?"

"Why don't you go back to the house, and we'll discuss it when I finish my run? Unless you want to join me?"

Her lips formed a moue of disgust. "Are you kidding? The only time I run is for a fifty-percent-off sale at the discount stores."

She flashed him a slow wink, then walked back toward the A-frame.

April strolled through the forest, her conscience clearer than it had been since their standoff began. She was becoming darned good at this apology stuff. Well, heck, she was getting plenty of practice. These past few days, she'd really gone overboard with the attitude, taking out her frustrations on the only other occupant in the house.

Fortunately, Jeff didn't hold a grudge. It was amazing that he'd turned out to be the good guy in this farce. Even while she froze him with icy looks, Jeff maintained an air of politeness. *Oh, sure, chalk up some of that facade to his "infinite acts of love and consideration."*

But face facts, April. You made it awfully hard for him to be nice to you, yet he never snapped. He never hurled an insult at you, even when you deserved one. And you deserved them lots of times, kiddo.

In *All About Eve,* Bette Davis said, "We're all busy little bees, full of stings, making honey day and night."

April guessed Bette had never met anyone like Jeff. The man

didn't seem to have a mean bone in his body. It was frustrating, really. No matter how nasty she became, Jeff maintained that calm veneer.

She had to give him kudos. The guy was her hero. And he topped off his other knight-in-shining-armor moments with his conversation with David earlier. If David had confronted *her,* she probably would have told him off and made things worse. But Jeff managed to explain their discomfort, and that confession had a positive effect: a whole weekend without the cameras monitoring every eyelash flutter.

Giddy with the thought, she struggled to keep her feet from dancing across the pine-needle floor. No cameras translated to a weekend during which she could relax her guard but still leave their next interview without fodder.

Imagine: a Monday without Grant and Jocelyn's twisting some innocent remark or action into drama. No catty remarks or exaggerated reactions from the audience. She could only imagine what those two would find to talk about on Monday morning. Based on past experience, she figured they'd rehash some episode from the first week—just to milk every drop of bad karma out of her behavior that they could.

She despised them, with their pursuit of ratings at any cost. And she despised David too. What a weasel. All smiles to April's face, but behind the scenes, he sliced and spliced their interactions to earn the biggest titillation factor. If he ever left television, he could always try his hand as a pimp. There wasn't much difference between TV broadcasting and prostitution.

Hadn't Jeff tried to warn her? Well, he shouldn't have any fear about her falling for television's poisoned apple. Once these thirty days ended, she'd return home and, if at all possible, fade back into obscurity. The media would never get her soul.

Chapter Twenty-four

After dinner, Jeff set up the Scrabble board while April loaded the dishwasher.

"What say we make the game a little more interesting?" he asked as he flipped the wooden tiles one by one inside the box cover.

Finished with her task, she dried her hands on a dish towel near the sink. Suspicion rang a little alarm bell in her ears, but she squelched it quickly. Without the cameras recording anything, why would he try to trap her?

"What do you mean? A bet or something?"

"Sort of."

She raised an eyebrow. "Define 'sort of.'"

"The loser has to do one thing the winner wishes."

A grin stretched her cheeks. "You mean like if I win, you have to cook dinner tomorrow?"

He shrugged. "If that's what you want."

If that was what she wanted? She had to admit that the idea held appeal. The taste of his beef burgundy still lingered on her palate. Or maybe the taste of the Shiraz lingered? Whatever. With the gauntlet thrown, April wouldn't hesitate to pick it up.

"You're on," she said, slapping the dish towel on the counter.

She headed into the living room and sat before the game board, then retrieved one of the slender wooden trays. Jeff had turned over all the tiles, and she reached into the box to pull out her first seven letters.

Her eyes scanned the results while her heart sank into her shoes. *Terrific. S, E, A, K, I, O,* and *D.* She was off to a flying start. The best she could do with this arrangement was to make a bunch of four-letter words. *Soda, side, dose, disk, skid, soak,* or *sake.* Yup, the possibilities were endless.

Her teeth sank into her lower lip as she reviewed her options. She probably should have clarified that "loser has to do what the winner wants" bit before agreeing. That was her fault for thinking herself some kind of Scrabble champion. Well, now she had to pray that his letters reeked more than hers.

When she peered at him over her tiles, her teeth forgot about her lips and bit her tongue instead. The frown marring his features lent credence to her hope of having a fighting chance.

"Do you want to go first?" he asked.

Feigning smugness, she flashed him a big cheesy grin. "Sure. Why not?"

Her fingers tickled across the tiles, allowing him time to wonder if she had a multitude of choices from which to decide. Well, she did have a lot of words to choose from. So what if those choices stank? He didn't have to know that.

She fiddled with the tiles a little longer, rearranging the letters into various patterns. *S-K-I, A-S-K. No, wait a minute. S-O-A-K-E-D.* Not a perfect choice, but it used the largest number of letters she could.

"Ahem!" Jeff's prompt startled her, and she nearly fell out of the chair.

"All right, all right," she grumbled, then grabbed the tiles and placed them on the board. "Let's see. That's six, nine, double letter score on the 'D' makes thirteen, and double the score because it's on the star. That gives me twenty-six points."

Not a bad opener after all. Victorious, she glanced up at Jeff and wished she hadn't. His eyes took on a wolfish glint as he spread his tiles on the board. He started near her *D* and quickly added *E, S, I, R, E,* and *S.*

His sultry eyes swept over her suddenly overheated figure as he murmured, "'Desires.' Sixteen points."

With shaking hands, she wrote both figures on the pad at her side, then reached for six more letters to go with her remaining *I.* She drew an *H,* two *E*s, an *N,* an *A,* and an *L.*

Okay, here goes nothing.

"The open 'S,'" she said, arranging her letters. "'H,' 'I,' 'N,' and 'E.' 'Shine.' With the double letter score on 'H,' that's twelve points."

Twelve points? Jeez, she'd better come up with something like *zygote* soon, or she'd find herself catering to Jeff's wish tonight.

And God only knew what he'd ask for.

Jeff barely hesitated before placing his next word on the board. "'Gazes,'" he said, "as in, 'When she *gazes* into my eyes, the world tilts on its side, and I lose all sense of balance.'"

She cocked her head at him. "You're kidding, right?"

"Of course not," he said with a lazy grin. "That's a perfectly good sentence."

"It is, if you're planning to write greeting cards," she retorted. "Besides, I didn't ask you for an example of the word use. I know perfectly well what 'gazes' means." She added up his tiles and wrote down his score.

The game continued for over an hour. April came up with innocuous words, like *joy, quote,* and *filet.* Jeff's word choices, however, bordered on suggestive in her opinion. *Taste, curve,* and *lips* were among his.

You're being ridiculous, she told herself. *He's playing the letters he has, just as you are. He can't possibly cheat at the game. Your attraction is getting the better of you.*

But dang, his aftershave smelled delicious. Her sensitive nostrils picked up a subtle hint of citrus they hadn't noticed before. She glanced at the board, and the word *evoke* leaped out at her. That was exactly what his scent did to her: evoked visions of lying beneath a hot sun while Jeff rubbed coconut oil over her bikini-clad body; evoked memories of his lips pressed against hers; evoked desires she'd long thought dead inside.

"Did you really lose jobs because you had to stay home with a sick child?"

His question shook her out of her reverie. "Huh?"

"On the show, you said I didn't know true responsibility because I never got fired for staying home with a sick child once too often. How many times did that happen to you?"

"Too many to count." Was he trying to trick her somehow? Well, he wouldn't break her concentration with this game the way he had during Parcheesi. "I can't tell you how often I weeded through abandoned lots for pop bottles to redeem for grocery money."

"Didn't your husband pay child support?"

"Not until the court ordered him to."

"Wow." He whistled through his teeth. "How did you manage?"

"You know how I managed," she replied in a cool tone. "We've discussed it before, remember?"

"We didn't discuss it in detail. What kind of jobs did you have?"

She shrugged. "Anything I could find."

"Like what? What was the worst job you ever had?"

Ha! An easy one. She even remembered the dates: March through May of 2004. "I worked on a mushroom farm."

"You didn't." His skepticism mixed with astonishment.

"Mmm-hmm. For about three months. It was awful. Freezing cold—even indoors."

"So what did you do there?"

She bit her lip and ran a finger over her wooden tiles. "Trust me. You don't wanna know."

"Yes, I do. What kind of work would you do on a mushroom farm? You didn't dig up the darned things, did you?"

"You don't dig them up," she replied. "You pick them. The picking season runs about eight weeks, and yes, I did pick mushrooms for those eight weeks. On my hands and knees, in the smelliest mud you could imagine."

"And what does a mushroom-picker make?"

She offered him a bitter smile. "I got three fifty an hour."

His lips twisted in a grimace. "Then why on earth would you do something like that?"

"To buy macaroni and cheese to feed my kids. We can't all afford personal chefs to hide in our closets," she snapped, then turned her attention back to the game board.

While her insides simmered, her shaking fingers pulled four letters off her tray and set them on the board near an open *O*. *I-D-I-O-T.* Only six points, but the most satisfying six points of the evening. And it got rid of two of her *I*s. All in all, a rewarding endeavor.

Jeff stared at the game board, but the letters refused to permeate his brain. Nothing could break through the wall of self-recriminations bottled up inside.

Finally, the word she'd created filtered in. *Idiot.* Well, she was right, wasn't she? The word fit him perfectly. He looked up into her face and saw the righteous anger darkening her eyes.

"If you could lend me an extra 'R,'" he said in a soft tone, "I might write 'sorry.'"

The anger fled her face and was replaced by surprise. "You *are* doing it on purpose, aren't you?"

He feigned an innocent newborn's face, admitting nothing.

She rolled her eyes and sighed in exasperation. "You're deliberately choosing provocative words. Why?"

"Provocative words?"

Her cheeks turned bright pink. "You know what I mean. Lips, curve, taste, gazes. All words meant to bring a certain mood to the game."

"Oh, come on, April. You don't really believe that, do you?"

She turned her attention to the fireplace. "I don't know what I believe."

"I didn't mean to make you so uptight. Let's forget about the wager."

Her gaze swerved to him again. "Oh, no, you don't. Just because I'm winning doesn't mean you can turn tail and run, you big coward."

He placed a hand over his heart. "Coward? *Moi?* Perish the thought. I thought I'd frightened *you* off."

Her eyes glinted beneath the overhead light fixture, flashing a golden challenge at him. "Never."

"Glad to hear it. Let's forget about ulterior motives and take the game seriously, then, shall we?"

"Aha!" She nearly upended the table in her exuberance. Several tiles scattered, and Jeff reached across the board to reset them. "You're admitting you had an ulterior motive."

Wow. Talk about a dog with a bone . . . The hungriest dog had nothing on April Raine. He shook his head. "You don't give up, do you?"

"Me? I'm not the one attempting seduction through Scrabble."

Hoping to cover his guilt, he tossed his head and laughed. "Is that a new game show?"

Her narrowed eyes suggested she didn't find any humor in his remark.

"Okay, so the jig is up. Too bad you caught on before the game could get really interesting. Now we'll have to settle for innocuous conversation. Tell me, what made you decide to agree to this challenge?"

"Wh-what?"

His mellow voice turned staccato. "Why are you here? And for that matter, why am I here? If you had turned down the challenge when the network first approached you, we both could have been safely at home, carefree and relaxed, right now. I think you owe me an explanation. And I'd love to hear it. Now."

Chapter Twenty-five

Only a moment earlier, Jeff had flashed a warm smile. In the time it had taken her to process his television game show analogy, the channel had changed from *Friends* to WWE. Now his lips disappeared behind a resentful frown, leaving April with a chill deep in her bones.

Fine, so fun time was over. No problem.

Pushing away from the table, she gave back glare for glare. "I had very little choice, if you must know. There were one hundred thousand reasons for me to go along with this stupid challenge."

"That's why you did this? For the money?" He smirked. "Wow. Who knew the Mother of the Year could be bought so easily?"

"What would you know about being bought? You've had it easy. Daddy's a captain of industry, and your wife was a television star! You've never had to scramble to pay a debt in your life."

"So what's the catch? Are you indebted to a bunch of loan sharks or something?"

"Or something."

"What?" She looked away, but he grabbed her chin and forced her gaze back to his intense silver scrutiny. "Tell me."

His eyes drew her in, but she fisted her hands at her sides, digging her fingernails into her palms and focusing on the pain. Let him think what he wanted. Hadn't he called her mercenary at their first meeting? Fine. So be it. She'd live with the title if she had to.

"Come on, April. What would possess you to sign up for this

exquisite purgatory? You couldn't possibly need money that badly. Grant and Jocelyn were touting you as a success story."

"Grant and Jocelyn don't know everything. They think because Rainey-Day-Wife is finally starting to show a profit in this fiscal year that I've suddenly become the female Donald Trump. Well, guess what? I'm going to need more than one year's profits to break even. I do have debts to pay."

"What kind of debts?" he demanded. "What don't Grant and Jocelyn know? You have gambling debts?"

She snorted and pushed to her feet.

"A drug problem?" he suggested next.

"Yup, that's it. I'm an addict." She raked fingers across her scalp. "You know how it is. You start out with those little orange baby aspirin, because they taste so good. Next thing you know, you're strung out at the local pharmacy, jonesing for your next tab of salicylic acid."

Despite his sitting while she stood, he managed to glare up at her with enough venom to make her squirm. "Forget the put-ons, April. What's going on in your life that would make you go to such extremes?"

"None of your business, Doctor."

"What is it?" His tone grew soft, deceptive, almost hypnotic in its cadence.

Oh, no. She would not fall for his psychobabble. On one long, deep inhale, she steeled her spine and folded her arms over her chest. To protect her heart? Her lungs failed her, refusing to exhale the breath she'd drawn.

"April, come on," he said in that same soothing voice. "Tell me. Make me understand."

"I need the money for medical bills, if you must know."

His eyes widened. Good, she'd surprised him. Nothing like keeping a man on his toes. All those old movie dowagers she loved must be watching her and beaming with pride right now.

"Are you sick?" he asked.

"A little too late to exhibit concern, Doc, but, hey"—her voice took on the tone of a game show host's—"thanks for playing our game. We have a nice consolation prize for you backstage."

She walked toward the picture window in the living room, all thoughts of games and wagers drowned in an ocean of questions about Michael. Was he okay? Could she trust that weasel David to come for her if something happened to either of her kids? Or would he take his sweet time returning here so the producers could pump up the ratings with her private agony?

For all she knew, Michael was already upset with her, wondering why his mom wasn't home by his side. Talk about an error in judgment . . . What kind of mother abandoned her children to appear on some twisted television show—for money?

"April?"

She didn't have to turn around to know that Jeff stood right behind her—even before he rested his hands on her shoulders. Thank God his aftershave gave him away every time. Otherwise she'd have no way of knowing when he'd moved so close. The man probably floated on air. The angel of psychology.

"April," he said softly. "Are you ill?"

"I'm fine." She shrugged away from his touch. The last thing she wanted from him was comfort. He didn't have the right. Besides, she preferred anger coursing in her veins to fear and guilt for Michael. "Don't worry about me."

"That's right," he said flatly. "You wouldn't be so upset if *you* were the sick one. That's not your style. So whose illness would upset you this way? Is it one of your children?"

Close. Too close. "Drop it. Forget I mentioned anything."

"Why? You think I won't understand?"

"I don't care if you understand or not. It's none of your business."

"You're a regular lioness when it comes to your kids, you know that? All sharp claws and angry roars."

"Someone has to be." The moment the words left her mouth, she wished she could take them back. Always too late.

"Your ex-husband's not?"

She definitely did not plan to bring Peter into this mess. "You know what Bette Davis said? 'Psychoanalysis. Almost went three times—almost. Then I decided what was peculiar about me was probably what made me successful.' "

"Dennis Miller said, 'Even the best psychiatrist is like a blindfolded auto mechanic poking around under your hood with a giant foam *We're #1* finger.' "

Despite her best efforts, a snicker escaped. Determined to give him no leeway, she fisted her hands and froze her facial muscles into a frown.

Outside, heavy storm clouds gathered, darkening the room and changing the atmosphere to ominous, perfectly timing her mood.

"Could we change the subject, please?"

"Talk to me, April."

Ready to blast him with outrage, she whirled around and nearly punched him in the nose. If he stood any closer, he could view the contents of her back pocket from inside. "Will you stop hovering around me? Why can't you leave me alone?"

"For one thing, because there's only two of us in this house. And for another, whatever's bothering you won't go away if you keep brooding."

"Spoken like a true psychologist."

He actually had the nerve to grin, as if she'd meant that as a compliment. "Occupational hazard, I'm afraid."

"Yeah, well, take a vacation for now, okay?"

Any minute she'd start bawling, and she couldn't allow him to see her weakest moment. With a grunt, she faced the window again and fought to regain control of the thunderstorm brewing inside her. A flock of birds communed on the branches of the nearby trees, confirming her suspicion that a major storm brewed outside too.

A tremor shook her shoulders, filtering through her torso to her knees. Oh, God, the tears now skated the brims of her eyes, and she had no ready plan to keep them in check. No Bette Davis lines, no platitudes about strength in the face of adversity, nothing came to mind to prevent her from making a fool of herself.

When the first tear began its journey down her cheek, strong arms enfolded her. She stiffened, but Jeff continued to simply hold her, never speaking. Her bones melted, leaving her in a pool of warm liquid. How long had it been since anyone had held her in a comforting way?

"Don't fight," he murmured, turning her until her face lay buried in his shirtfront. "Just let go."

As if his words had power, she collapsed into a blubbering mess. Whispered hushes wafted to her ears while he embraced her and rocked her back and forth with the motion of a parent lulling an infant to sleep.

How long had it been? Too long since she'd felt so safe, so secure, so . . . cared for.

From the moment she'd discovered she was pregnant with Becky, April had been forced to play the strong, stoical role. Her parents— Lord, for the longest time, they reacted as if a surprise pregnancy had the same impact as leprosy.

And Peter, like the Pan, refused to grow up. All the years of their marriage, she'd been the rock, the dynamic that had kept their partnership on an even keel. She'd paid the bills and "made do." Her husband never understood financial matters, couldn't fathom the idea of tightening his belt when money was scarce. Nor did he handle any of the other serious issues that cropped up in their family.

She had stayed up with sick kids, helped with homework, held little hands during immunizations at the doctor's office, fought with school administrators, confronted the stares and gawks of strangers. Even now, with Becky away at college, who still fretted if more than a day went by without a phone call? Not Peter—no, never Peter. He couldn't even back her up about their daughter's not attending a rock concert in a bar.

Peter wanted to be Dad only for the accolades, leaving April to fill the role of Bad Guy.

Perhaps that was why Jeff's simple interaction affected her so deeply. After years of her playing the hardnose, the solid, reliable one, at long last someone allowed her to fall apart. With his granted permission, a dam burst inside her, and her flood of tears saturated his shirt.

She cried for Michael and for Becky, for the lean years, for the betrayals, for the blows to her pride, for every worrisome minute she'd endured since the day her adolescence ended and adulthood began. Her hands fisted inside the folds of Jeff's shirt while she vented years of frustrations and disappointments in gut-wrenching sobs. She cried until nothing remained inside her.

Hollowed, she pulled away and stared up at him. Gratitude and relief washed over her in soft undulating waves.

"Better now?" he asked.

She nodded.

"Good. Because I'm going to need to change my clothes."

Giggles in the form of hiccups erupted from her lips. "I'm—hic!—sorry—hic!—about that."

"Forget it. From now on, I won't have to worry about doing my own laundry. I'll just let you cry all over me." His smile dimmed, and he cocked his head to one side slightly. "Out of curiosity, though, you want to tell me what that was all about?"

Ice encased her, snapping her back to rigidity. Her fists left his shirtfront to retain their positions at her sides. "No."

"Okay. Have it your way."

He left her in front of the window and sat on the couch, feigning concentration on his perfectly manicured fingernails. April didn't buy into his nonchalance. No matter where he focused his eyes, his resentment filled the room like a solid brick wall. It closed her off from him, from the comfort he'd offered mere seconds before. Guilt twitched at her already jumpy nerves.

He'd called her a lioness. Was she really that ferocious? Maybe. She readily admitted that her children meant everything to her. Television viewers might have trouble believing that, but April knew the truth. If selling herself would keep her kids safe and financially secure, she'd put herself on the auction block a thousand times a day.

A sigh escaped her lips. Once again, Jeff had extended an olive branch toward her, and she'd snapped it in half. And once again, she'd have to swallow her pride to make amends.

Her legs trembled as she took those first tentative steps toward him. He looked up, his facial muscles relaxed.

A doorway opened in their invisible wall, allowing her to walk through and sit beside him. Intense longing rose inside her, a desire to have his arms around her again. Well, she'd have to repair the damage she'd done first.

It's now or never, April.

"My son." The words stuck in her throat like a dry chicken bone. With a loud "ahem," she tried again. "M-Michael is a child with Down syndrome."

Chapter Twenty-six

He blinked. Other than that, she saw no reaction to the confession that fractured her heart almost daily.

The memories rushed through her brain at lightning speeds, a crosscut of misery: the joy of clearing the first trimester after many miscarriages, the excitement of decorating a nursery, the pile of name books on her night table, Becky talking to the baby in her belly before bedtime, her first labor pains, and the somber expression on the face of her obstetrician when his suspicions were confirmed through karyotype.

The moment she disclosed the news to family and friends, she saw her own shock and disappointment mirrored in their faces.

Every emotion of those early days renewed itself in vivid detail.

"Complications?" Jeff asked, dragging her into the present.

She shook her head. "In that respect, Michael's very lucky. No heart problems. So far, his vision is fine and there's been no sign of hypothyroidism or"—she swallowed another chicken bone—"leukemia."

"Well, that's encouraging. Down syndrome's not a death sentence, you know. There's no reason why your son can't live a fairly normal life."

"I know." Typical medical mumbo jumbo. "But I'm his mother. I can't help worrying, thinking about the future, dreading what might happen."

"And Michael's father . . . ?" The question trailed off, but April understood what Jeff asked.

"Peter's never really been comfortable with the idea that his only son isn't 'normal.'" She held up a hand, stemming any comment Jeff might want to add. "Don't get me wrong. Peter loves Michael, but in short spurts. On his terms. You know what I mean?"

She waited a beat until he nodded.

"I think if the decision had been left to him, Peter would have put Michael in an institution years ago."

"So you're Michael's only champion," he noted.

A knot of fear blocked her throat, and she coughed to dislodge the lump. "Yet I abandoned him to strangers to pursue this stupid challenge."

"You left your son with his father," he pointed out.

"No, I didn't. Peter only has him for the first two weeks. He and his new wife will be off on their second honeymoon cruise next week."

Jeff shifted in his seat, and his brow furrowed in disbelief. "He couldn't wait until this month was over?"

"The rates go up next month, you know." A bitter laugh escaped. "Peter's more childish than either of his kids. And I knew that. I've always known that. I should have known better than to trust him when he told me he'd take care of Michael for the month. A full month's way past his comfort zone."

"Who's going to watch him for the rest of the time?"

"My assistant's mother. She's a retired rehab therapist. And Michael likes her. More important, I like her. I trust her. Still . . . you were right. I must be some kind of mercenary to care so little for my family that I'd abandon them for a month for money."

"April, I couldn't name another mother who cares so much for her family."

"Oh, right." She snorted, then sniffed. Tears poured down her cheeks. "What if something happens to me?" The question came out a harsh whisper, but she pressed on, vocalizing every terror she'd faced since Michael's birth. "Who'd take care of my son? Not Peter. And Becky's way too young to shoulder that kind of responsibility. What if something happens to Michael while I'm here? I wouldn't even know about it. Maybe not until it was too late."

Thunder boomed, rattling the window, and April flinched.

Naturally, Jeff never reacted to the loud crash. His posture—one leg across the other as he watched her closely, probably discerning reasons for every motion she made—reflected the eternal competent psychoanalyst. If she were to fold her arms over her chest right now, would he assume that meant she was hiding something? Surreptitiously, she slid her hands beneath her bottom to prevent such an action.

"I'm sure David would arrange for you to leave immediately if something serious should happen to your kids."

She frowned. "*Are* you? Because I'm not."

"David's young and ambitious, but he's not an ogre."

"Well, I've yet to see his warm and fuzzy side."

"I never said he was warm and fuzzy. Just human."

Fine hairs bristled on her neck. "Yeah, right. As human as cold spaghetti."

"He's young. I doubt he's any different than most guys under the age of thirty. You remember that time in your life, don't you? Not a care in the world, no one to worry about but yourself . . ."

She cocked her head, eyes narrowed. "You're kidding, right?"

"Sorry," he mumbled. "Of course not. But most young men—and women, for that matter—shirk responsibility for a lot longer nowadays. David's completely unaware of what you have on your plate, that's all."

"Mmm." She tilted her head against the couch and stared up at the dark wooden crossbeams overhead. "Maybe."

"You know what your problem is?"

Her head came down with a snap so forceful her spine twinged. "We're not finished listing my inadequacies yet?"

"You have no inadequacies, April." He rose from the couch and stood over her. "None that I've discovered, anyway. The people that surrounded you all your life are the guilty ones. They've let you down."

For the briefest moment, she tried to conjure up a defense for her parents, but bitter memories squelched her attempts. Staring out the window, April didn't really see the storm, the tree branches whipping in the wind, or the rain streaming down the glass. What she saw was a hospital room from more than a decade earlier.

"When Michael was born," she said, her tone husky with resentment, "I was in a ward room in maternity. It was huge, with four beds rather than the usual two you find in semiprivate rooms. But oddly enough, I guess the hospital was kind of slow that week, because I had that room all to myself. So it was almost as if I had a private room, you know? At the time, my husband was working double shifts, so he could only come to the hospital sporadically. My in-laws were taking care of my daughter, and they'd bring her every afternoon after school for a while. But at night . . ."

Tears spilled from her eyes, rolling down her cheeks the way the rainwater rolled down the glass.

"What happened at night?" There was no urgency in his prompt, merely curiosity, she supposed.

The answer nearly choked her when she brought it up from her scarred heart. "No one came. Not my parents, not my sisters. Here I had this huge room with plenty of space for visitors or flowers or baby gifts, and no one showed up. Ever. It was like they'd written Michael off already. Every night I'd hear laughter coming from the room next door, or I'd see the crowds of proud grandparents and aunts and uncles cramming around the nursery window to get a look at their newest family member. But no one was there for me and Michael. I didn't even get a congratulations card. God, you have no idea how much that hurt."

Pain crested in waves, lifting her pounding heart into her throat, then sinking it beneath an ocean of repressed rage.

"I realized then," she said above the roar in her ears, "I would have to be the hero in my family drama. No one would give me support or encouragement. If I wanted Michael to have any chance at a normal life, I'd have to make it happen for him. By myself."

He knelt before her, cupped the frigid fingers of her right hand inside his warm palm. "And because of instances like those, episodes of familial neglect and selfishness, you learned to put too much pressure on your shoulders," he summed up. "If you have any flaw at all, April, it's that you don't know how to ask for help."

Fiery ice licked her cheeks and crackled downward, racking her body with shivers. Just when she believed she'd break into a million pieces, he stood and pulled her upright, their faces mere inches apart. His hands clasped behind her back, locking her in his embrace.

Warm breath brushed her cheek while his aftershave, that same clove and citrus fragrance she'd grown to expect, surrounded her like an aromatic cloud. His face, all angles and planes, inched closer to her throat. She swallowed. An incredible thirst burned inside while she stared at his moist lips. The longing to be held returned with ferocity, an overwhelming desire to allow Jeff's arms to support her, to embrace her with passion—even temporarily.

One small molecule in her brain remained sane, screaming a warning to be careful what she wished for. April barely heard and certainly didn't heed the alert over the billion needy molecules drowning out such a weak argument.

Battered on emotional rocks after the last few hours, she just plain didn't have the strength to communicate her request. A courageous woman might take matters into her own hands, or mouth, as the case might be. April, however, lacked that quality. Too bad all her movie heroines were dead. Any one of them would know what to do in this situation.

Unbidden, her tongue flicked out to lick her arid lips. As if the action communicated some secret message to Jeff, his mouth came down on hers.

It was heaven, sheer heaven.

What about this man affected her so drastically? No one else had ever weakened her resolve, filled her senses, and awakened every ounce of her dormant femininity. Nothing in life had prepared her for the hypnotic trance this man cast.

His tongue, feather light, traced her lips—first the upper, then the lower. When his teeth grazed the same lines, pleasure rippled down her spine. She shivered, and his arms enveloped her.

She swayed on her feet, and he moved his mouth to her throat, murmuring, "I think you need to lie down."

"No!" She clung to his neck like a drowning woman. "Don't leave me. Please."

He smiled. "I meant *we* need to lie down. If that's what you want."

"Yes," she sighed, surrendering to the hot bliss suffusing every pore.

Straightening, he took her hand. "Come on."

Spellbound, she allowed him to lead her down the hallway and into the bedroom.

Despite the darkness, Jeff led April to the twin mattress on her side of the bedroom with little effort. Once there, he didn't bother turning on a light. Instead, with one quick yank, he pulled the blankets back.

"In," he ordered her.

Sidling against him, she nuzzled his neck. "Only if you're coming with me."

"Fair enough," he said.

"Good." She sat on the edge of the bed and kicked off her shoes. "I can't think of a better way to spend a stormy evening."

Once her shoes hit the floor, he knelt and grasped her ankles. Before she could guess his intentions, he had her tucked in beneath the covers. "I'm glad. Now get some sleep."

"Oh." Her disappointed tone made him smile, and he thanked God he hadn't shed any light in the room. She probably wouldn't have understood his delight.

Her offer tempted him, though not enough for him to take her up on it. Right now her need for human contact—to cling to someone and receive comfort—overrode all her common sense. Jeff, however, suffered no such delusion.

Oh, he wanted her—so much it hurt. Still, better he hurt now than she hurt tomorrow.

Thunder boomed, and April flinched. "Jeff?" Panic laced the question.

"Hmmm?"

"You'll stay with me, won't you?"

He slid next to her, remaining atop the blankets. She scooched up against him, one hand resting on his chest. Satisfied she'd stay put, he pulled her closer and kissed the top of her head. "Where would I go? Now get some sleep."

"What are you thinking?"

"I'm thinking you should go to sleep."

"No," she snorted. "Really."

"If I tell you, will you go to sleep?"

"I'll try."

"I'm thinking that you're the most frustrating, stubborn, amazing woman I've ever met."

She sighed. "That's nice."

Lightning glowed around the room for a fraction of a second, then fled. In the momentary light, he studied her eyes, swollen but closed. Apparently, she was losing the battle to stay awake. Good. That would make his place here beside her easier to bear.

"Jeff?"

"Hmmm?"

"Wanna know what I'm thinking?"

"Not unless you're thinking about sleep."

She giggled. "Of course not. I'm thinking I'm glad I told you about Michael."

"I'm glad you told me too."

She fell asleep a few minutes later. Jeff, on the other hand, stayed awake through the night, listening to the rage of nature outside their windows.

For the first time in six years, thoughts of Emma didn't haunt him in the dark. Rather, one inevitable truth shone brighter than a thousand suns inside his head. April had supplanted Emma in his heart.

And Jeff never wanted to let her go.

Chapter Twenty-seven

April woke with a raging headache and deadweight limbs. When she tried to roll over, the blankets refused to budge. *What the . . . ?*

She opened one eye—and saw Jeff beside her, a goofy smile on his face.

"Oh my God!" Disbelief gave her the strength of Atlas, and she kept kicking at the wrappings until she fought her way clear of the cocoon of blankets. With her feet on solid ground, she whirled to confront Jeff. "Get out of my bed. Now."

He never flinched. He still wore that insipid grin, and his eyes crinkled with delight. "And a cheery good morning to you too."

"Did I . . . Did we . . . ? What happ—" Shame closed her throat, leaving her unable to voice her fears aloud.

"Relax. I was a perfect gentleman." He waggled his brows at her. "Despite the fact you made me several tempting offers."

"I did not!"

But a tiny voice inside her refuted her denial. Oh, dear God, had she? Memories trickled into her head drip by enlightening drip: David's departure, their bizarre Scrabble game, followed by her baring her soul and, sweet saints, inviting him to lie beside her in this bed.

Realization sparked a wildfire across the back of her neck, to her hairline. But worse, much worse, worst of all, she'd told him about Michael. Of all the boneheaded things to do . . .

She wasn't ashamed of her son—not at all. Her concern lay in Jeff's possibly using that information as a weapon. Look what he'd done when she'd told him about Peter. And while no real damage had occurred because of his transgression, who knew if she could count on that sort of luck a second time?

"If you say one word to anyone about Michael, I swear—"

"Ah, there's my lioness." The words were smoother than vanilla ice cream. He shifted his position on her bed, back against the wall, totally at ease. Through his maneuverings, the grin remained. The fire at her hairline crackled down her spine, pooling in her stomach and churning the acid already residing there. She swallowed a burning gulp.

"I'm serious, Jeff. My kids are off-limits. Do you understand me?"

At last the smile disappeared, and he blinked. "I don't know whether to be amused or insulted by that edict."

"Take it any way you like," she snapped, "so long as the end result is you keep your mouth shut."

"No problem."

He didn't smile, but his banal tone suggested he patronized her. Why? So he could outwit her somehow?

"I mean it, Jeff."

"I know you do. Now, would you stop indulging murderous fantasies about me so we can have an intelligent conversation?"

Of course. He planned to outwit her with words. Too bad he wouldn't get the chance. She refused to allow him to get the upper hand in this discussion. He might have the college degree and the people skills, but she had right on her side.

"I'm not discussing anything with you. Not until you promise what I told you about Michael yesterday stays between you and me."

The grin returned. "Scout's honor."

She wanted to scream the ceiling down on his arrogant head. Instead, she turned and fled the room.

"April!"

Jeff's summons followed her down the stairs, but she didn't stop. She flew past the living room, out the front door, and down the porch. Last night's storm had left the ground muddy, and April had forgotten to put on her shoes, but she didn't care. She needed air, needed to think, preferably somewhere far away from a certain smirking psychologist.

Mud gave way to bits of gravel, and despite sharp pricks to her tender insteps, she kept moving. She crossed the tree line and plunged into the thickest part of the woods, then stopped, transfixed. No more than ten yards ahead, her fawn stood with its mother, bent over the clear running stream.

Michael, her heart cried. She must have sobbed aloud, because both deer raised their heads and scampered away. Alone again, she remained still and allowed her thoughts to flow like the nearby stream.

Maybe she should take a page from the mama deer—cut and run. She'd given this Harmony House challenge her best shot. As much as she'd sell herself for her kids' sakes, she'd never turn the tables to make a buck. She'd made lots of mistakes in her life, and she was willing to pay for them. Becky and Michael, however, were innocent bystanders. Becky was the product of a teenager's rebellion, and Michael was that same teenager's last-ditch effort to keep a bad marriage intact. They didn't deserve to have their lives placed under a national microscope.

"You are the most stubborn woman." Jeff's exasperated voice broke the stillness around and inside her.

"Go away," she ordered without turning around.

"Where is your coat?"

"Who cares?"

With a parent's righteous anger making her hotter than Hades, she had no need for a coat.

"No shoes either, I see," he added. "You have a death wish?"

"No, but *you* must, to keep pushing me."

"You're going to catch pneumonia out here. Tell me. When you're hospitalized, who's going to take care of Michael?"

She whirled then, facing him with all the rage she could bring up from her churning stomach. "You son of a—" The insult died in her throat when he held up her jacket and sneakers.

"I forgot socks," he admitted, "but you could at least slip these on for the walk back to the house."

Another peace offering. This time she wouldn't crumble under his act of consideration. "I had a daddy, Jeff, and my mom is still alive, so I'm really not looking for substitute parents at the moment."

"You should be." He dropped the jacket over her shoulders. "Because you surely deserved better parents than the ones you had."

"Yeah, well, if an opening becomes available, you can apply for the position, okay?" Surrendering to the cold, she shoved her arms into the puffy sleeves and zipped up. "Right now I want you to go away and leave me alone, okay?"

"No, not okay. You know, you may not want to hear this, but your parents did a poor job of raising you."

Her eyes narrowed. "Is that so?"

"If they didn't spend every waking moment of your life telling you how amazing you were, then, yes, that's so!"

In all their time together, she'd never heard him shout before. She added to his decibel level, though, the fact that his eyes looked at her with solemnity—without any mockery or humor. She refused to buy the act for a minute.

"You can turn off the sweet talk." She strode past him with as much grace as she could manage, considering her bare feet were numb from cold and coated with mud. "When David comes back Monday, I'll tell him it's over. You win the challenge. Put Rainey-Day-Wife on your stupid list every year for the next hundred years. I'm done. I'm leaving Harmony House. I never should have come here in the first place."

His hand shot out and grasped her elbow before she took more than a dozen steps. "You're not going anywhere."

She stopped, allowing her gaze to smolder from his hand to his face. "Excuse me?"

Releasing her, he pointed to a nearby fallen log. "Sit down and put your shoes on. I want to talk to you. If you still want to leave after what I have to say, I won't stop you."

He'd piqued her interest. He knew that much before she plopped down on the log. The angry flush left her cheeks, and her rigid posture softened.

Should he really open up to April? For years, he'd carried the burden alone, determined no one should learn the truth. Maybe he should forget about this confession, tell April she was free to leave, and keep his own counsel.

Her eyes, bright with curiosity and unshed tears, gave him the courage to go on. After taking a deep breath, he plunged into his story.

"I know you think by revealing Michael's condition to me, you've given me another weapon to use against you. But you really haven't. What you've given me is far greater. You've given me your trust. Now I want to return the favor."

She leaned forward, one arm bent across her abdomen, and simply waited for him to continue.

"What I'm about to tell you is strictly confidential." He paced back and forth across the pine-needle floor. "No one, and I mean no one, knows about this."

"Come on, Jeff!" April exclaimed, squirming. "Get on with it. My keister's getting wet sitting here. What do you want to tell me? You have a secret wish to join the circus? You found where I hid my pick-me-up spa stash and you want to borrow some?"

Surprise stopped him, and he stared at her. "No. But I may be interested in learning more about that pick-me-up spa stash later."

Her cheeks turned pink, but his own discomfort far overwhelmed any humor he found in hers. Guilt made him restless, and he resumed his strides to work off excess anxiety.

"I want to tell you about my marriage."

She shot to her feet. "You know what? I don't need to hear about that."

"Yes, you do." He brought a hand to her shoulder and pressed her to sit again. "Please."

The shoes dangling from her fingertips dropped to the ground with a thud. "O-okay."

"Emma and I married when I was still in residency. I had this drive in those days . . . I don't know." He scuffed his boot along a bed of dead pine needles until moist earth peeked up from the razor-thin fingers of tan. "It was inexcusable. Emma had already started work on *Tomorrow Is Another Day,* so money wasn't really much of an issue for us."

"There was probably more to your drive than money, Jeff. Don't forget, you'd given up the opportunity to fall into a very lucrative business with your father for the chance to do something on your own. Naturally, you'd want to succeed, if only to avoid hearing 'I told you so.' "

Redeemed by her understanding, he offered her a sad smile. "Something you're fairly familiar with, eh?"

She waved him off. "We've already covered my history. It's your turn in our spotlight without a spotlight, remember?"

He grimaced. "Right. Well, regardless of why I focused more on work than on my marriage, the result was the same. Emma started sliding away from me little by little."

The restlessness returned with a vengeance, and he paced at a frenetic rate. Back and forth, back and forth, like a caged rat on a caffeine high. Words tripped over his tongue in a race to get out of his mouth.

"I never knew, never noticed. I should have, I realize that now. If I'd been home more. If I'd paid more attention to what she was up to. Maybe I could've stopped her, saved her, saved Michael."

"Jeff, slow down. I can't follow you. What exactly are you saying? Save Michael from what?"

He paused, and his knees shook under the staggering weight of self-recrimination. "Not your Michael. My Michael. Michael was our son's name also. He lived for two minutes after birth. Then he just closed his eyes and died. . . ."

The vision of his tiny boy swam in his imagination, and he squeezed his eyes shut to force the memory away. One deep breath for fortitude and he finally gave voice to the secret he'd kept for too long.

"Emma had a problem. She didn't die of complications of childbirth. She died of complications brought on by her anorexia and addiction to diet pills."

Chapter Twenty-eight

April's breath left her in one sharp gasp. She'd read about su-permodels and actresses who starved themselves to keep their figures slim and popped diet pills to maintain the high energy needed for the spotlight. But those were images of people she didn't know, glossy photographs of strangers in supermarket tabloids. Until this moment, she'd never come so close to the devastation.

"Anorexic?" she managed to say through dry lips. "Your wife was anorexic?"

His expression grim, Jeff nodded. "She'd always been con-cerned about her weight, but once her role on that soap opera took off, she became obsessed with how she looked. 'The camera adds ten pounds' and all that nonsense. She was constantly dieting, working out, drinking gallons of coffee and water. Then she got pregnant. I assumed she'd stop worrying so much about her weight then, you know? I figured the producers would write her condition into the show, and she'd stop stressing about what should have been a happy event."

"But they didn't," April recalled. "So she didn't."

He sighed, and April imagined that the exhale released only a fraction of his pain. "The writers couldn't work her pregnancy into the script and still keep the current story line they had for her. But they promised they'd set scenes around her condition—dress her in baggy clothes, place her behind desks or seat her at a table so her belly wouldn't be noticeable . . ."

"So what happened?"

"I don't really know for certain. I think she was probably

already in trouble before the pregnancy. She worried that her face would look puffy, that people would find her appearance ridiculous, that the ratings would suffer. After all, she was supposed to be the sexy siren of Maplewood Park on *Tomorrow Is Another Day*. And as her pregnancy progressed, her symptoms worsened. I should have paid more attention to her." He scrubbed his face with his hands. "I attributed the mood swings and sleeplessness to changing hormones, and found excuses to be away from the house more and more when she started complaining. You should have seen her. She'd be ecstatic one minute, working with a decorator on the baby's nursery; then she'd start screaming that no one understood what she was going through, and she'd chase everybody out of the apartment. Even me. I never questioned it. Just took the coward's way out and left her alone. I still can't believe I did that. . . ."

He let his explanation trail off there. April suspected he sought some redemption from her, and she rose from the log to place an arm around his waist. "Jeff, you aren't responsible for her weakness—"

"I know," he interrupted with a wistful smile. "You taught me that."

"Me?"

He nodded. "Remember the night I didn't do the dishes while you were in the tub? I was thinking about something you'd said that day about your ex-husband."

Her gaze remained riveted on his face, the sadness in his eyes, the grim pallor of his cheeks. "Wh-what did I say?"

"That Peter's cheating was his weakness, not yours. And that nothing would stop him until he changed or"—his Adam's apple bobbed with a large swallow—"died."

Sharp pains racked her chest, and she backed away from him. "Oh, Jeff, I'm sorry. I didn't mean Emma—"

"Don't apologize. You were absolutely right. Maybe if I'd confided in someone before this, I might have figured that out sooner. And we wouldn't be in the mess we're in now."

"I'm not sure I understand. What does Emma's death have to do with me?"

Jeff cocked a brow at her. "Figure it out."

What was this—some kind of game show?

I'll take Cryptic Statements for five hundred, Alex.

Would she have asked the question if she already knew the answer? *No, wait.* One image floated free from her miasma of thoughts, and she blurted the words out quickly. "Your book."

A rueful smile twisted his lips. "Right as usual."

His confirmation only made her bolder, and she turned on him in disbelief. "You turned your private grief into a self-help book? How could you? And the list? The infamous list my company's topped every single year?"

He had the grace to flush. "My agent's idea—to help promote the book."

"Of course." She couldn't stifle the bitter laugh that erupted. She didn't want to stifle it.

"You're angry," he pointed out.

No kidding. Very observant of him.

"Why shouldn't I be? This may have been some kind of publicity stunt for you, but I put my life on hold and abandoned my kids for thirty days. And for what? For you to wallow in your so-called guilt to the delight of a national audience. Why didn't you just wear a hair shirt, Jeff? Or a little sackcloth-and-ashes number, maybe."

"There's nothing 'so-called' about my guilt."

"There's nothing concrete about it either," she snapped. "You didn't supply your wife with diet pills, and you certainly didn't force her to starve herself!"

Her temples throbbed with her outburst, and she took several deep, cleansing breaths before the tension eased.

"Bette Davis once said, 'The weak are the most treacherous of us all. They come to the strong and drain them. They are bottomless. They are insatiable. They are always parched and always bitter. They are everyone's concern and like vampires they suck our life's blood.' Your wife was weak, Jeff. She was your vampire."

"Do you always have to quote Bette Davis when you're upset?"

Ignoring his attempt to change the subject, she stared at the treetops that swayed in the overhead breeze. When she spoke again, her voice was soft and sorrowful. "I don't get you. Unless you've been putting on a great act for the last two weeks, you're the most perfect husband material I've ever met. If I were lucky enough to be married to someone like you, I'd spend my days thanking whatever fate brought you into my life. You'll forgive me for saying so, but your late wife was nothing more than a spoiled junkie. High on legal, over-the-counter stuff, but a junkie nonetheless. The sooner you accept that, the sooner you'll give up the martyr routine and go on with your life. You say I deserved better parents? I believe you deserved a better wife."

He leaned close, so close she smelled his citrus aftershave. "Someone like you, for instance?"

Heat filled her face, but she shook off her embarrassment and took a step away from his intoxicating scent. "I'd settle for someone who would appreciate how terrific a guy you really are. You know what *your* problem is?"

"No. Tell me."

"You're not satisfied being a psychologist. You want to be God." Without giving him a chance to form a reply, she turned and picked up her neglected shoes. "Now, I'm cold, I'm about to lose my toes to frostbite, and thanks to your keeping me on that log over there, my butt is soaked. I'm going back to the cabin to take a hot shower, change, and grab a cup of coffee. You're welcome to stay here and play around with the heavens. Maybe you can find a way to turn back time and change your fate and your wife's."

Before he could raise his slack jaw, she turned and stalked off. Feeling his eyes boring into her shoulder blades, she managed to keep her pace to a sedate walk until she turned the curve in the path that covered her from his view.

Inside, though, her furious sense of fairness warred to take control of her limbs. She wanted to kick something, punch something, bite something, take out her frustrations on one of those balloon clowns that she could knock down and have pop up over and over again.

Why did he have to tell her about his wife? That he'd wasted half a dozen years mourning a woman unworthy of such devotion enraged her. Maybe she should write a book to contradict his *Love Is a Contact Sport*. She'd call it *Love Is Hazardous to Your Health*.

Not that anyone would buy it. After all, who'd buy a self-help book from an author beyond help? Because despite what she knew about herself and about him, April had fallen head over heels in love with Jeff.

If she hadn't wept herself into dehydration last night while thinking of Michael, she'd have bawled right now for herself. Without tears as an outlet, her body released its aggressive emotions in bone-rattling shivers. Once again, she'd allowed her heart to overrule her head—with disastrous results.

Thank goodness Jeff hadn't fallen for her clumsy seduction the way she'd fallen for Peter's so many years ago.

Why would he? He still carried a torch for his anorexic wife. She winced, recalling her callous reaction to his confession. She blamed her aching heart, which had lashed out in self-defense.

The gravel walkway loomed, and she quickened her pace to cross the cruel stones with as little pain as possible. She took the steps at full speed and didn't stop until she'd reached the safety of the bathroom and locked the door. Minutes later, under the shower's needling spray, her tear ducts rejuvenated. April sank to the tub floor and wept herself dry yet again.

Chapter Twenty-nine

Jeff had decided to give April a wide berth when he returned. It wasn't a difficult thing to do, considering she was locked in the bathroom when he entered the house. Grateful for the chance to regain his bearings, he filled a cup with coffee from the pot in the kitchen, then moved into the dining room. He still needed time to think. Outside, he'd thought about nothing but ways to take the chill out of his bones. Counterproductive, to say the least.

Although he sat at the table staring into the steaming contents of his mug, he was fully aware of April's arrival and subsequent flutter around the kitchen. Curious about what she might do, he said nothing; he simply waited and watched through the doorway. She had immediately begun to wipe down spotless counters. And when the granite gleamed, she dusted the tops of appliances, apparently intent on banishing all dirt from her kingdom.

Jeff had lived with her long enough to comprehend that she used housework as her coping mechanism. With no need to worry that the cameras might portray him as lazy to a nationwide audience, he intended, this time, to let her wear herself out with her Ms. Clean routine.

After all, her distraction served his purposes—until she dragged a stool across the floor and climbed atop it to dust the ceiling-fan blades.

When she stood on tiptoes, the stool, unstable with one leg on a tile grout line, wobbled slightly.

"Watch it!" He slammed his coffee cup on the table and raced to grab her calves.

Her shriek nearly shattered his eardrums. "Are you crazy?"

"Are *you*?" he shot back, releasing her legs. "Get down from there right now before you break your neck."

"Gee, Jeff." She smirked and climbed off the stool. "I didn't know you cared."

The overhead light showed off the shadows under her red, swollen eyes with intensity.

"What's wrong with your eyes?"

"Nothing," she insisted, but she turned away from his scrutiny. "I got shampoo in them in the shower."

She was the lousiest liar he'd ever met. Obviously, she'd been crying. What he couldn't figure out was why. *He'd* just bared his soul to *her,* not the other way around. Annoyance buzzed inside him like a pesky mosquito, and he strode back to the dining room and his coffee before the buzzing grew too loud to ignore.

He'd barely lifted the mug to his lips before she collapsed into the chair across from him. "Jeff, can we talk?" She held up a hand in front of his face. "Not about any of the stuff we talked about already. I won't mention your wife if you don't mention my son, okay?"

"O-kay." Giving up on drinking hot coffee, he set the mug down again. "What should we talk about?"

"I don't know." Frowning, she slapped her hands on the glossy cherry surface. "I mean, over the last twelve hours, we've become totally intimate on one level, yet we're still strangers on another level. It's got me off balance." Her voice lowered to a mournful whisper. "I don't like being off balance. Reminds me too much of my marriage . . ."

His too, now that he thought about it. So she had a valid point. As usual.

"How about . . ." Her voice spilled out tentatively, almost shyly. "How about . . . for today . . . you and I act like two people who've just met?"

"You mean, like this is a first date? Where we ask each other getting-to-know-you kinds of questions like 'What's your favorite color?'"

"Yes." Her cheeks flared crimson, and he bit back an indulgent smile. "I mean, no. Not a first date, per se. But yes, to the simple getting-to-know-you kind of questions. I know it sounds stupid, but—"

"Green." Whatever discomfort filled her head right now, he wanted it cleared away before he popped his surprise on her. "What's yours?"

"Mine?"

"Your favorite color, remember?"

"Oh, right. Gray."

He cocked an eyebrow at her. "You're kidding."

"Nope."

"Gray? As in, not black, not white. *Gray*."

She nodded. "Is that so hard to believe?"

"Well, yes. I would've expected you to say pink or blue, or even purple, maybe. But gray? Is gray even a color?"

"It is in my world."

Now was not the time to psychoanalyze her. Frankly, he didn't have the energy. And he had something much more serious on his mind.

"Let's try a different topic. Mind if I ask you a question?"

"Depends on what it is."

He laughed, then quickly sobered and grabbed her hand before he lost his nerve. "Whose darling are you, April Raine?"

"Huh?" She shook her head as if she hadn't heard him correctly.

"Because I'd like you to be mine."

"Huh?" She blinked once, twice, three times, but still the words didn't penetrate. She couldn't have heard him correctly. "You want what?"

His laughter boomed across the dining room.

Yanking her hand away, she fixed him with a glare meant to blister. "Ha-ha. Very funny, Jeff."

One hand on the tabletop, she pulled herself out of the chair. *Jerk.* Here she tried to regain some sort of peace between them, but he wanted to play mind games instead—as usual. Well, she was done with games. She turned toward the kitchen, intent on reclaiming her perch on the stool.

Steel arms wrapped around her waist and stopped her in mid-step. "Oh, no, you don't. You are *not* going to walk away from what I just said to conquer imaginary dirt demons in the kitchen."

Tears skimmed her lower lids. God, she would have expected to be cried out by now, but apparently something about Jeff left her with an endless supply of waterworks.

Sniffing them back as best she could, she craned her neck to look into his face, so close his whiskers abraded her cheek. "You're a jerk, you know that?"

He had the nerve to smile. "Maybe. But I'm pouring out my heart to you. The least you can do is reciprocate. Is it possible you like me—maybe a little?"

Whatever he planned to serve her, she refused to bite. "Cute."

Why did he have to torment her like this? They only had to get through ten more days. Ten more days and they'd go their separate ways. Ten more days and she could bury herself in work. Ten more days and she'd begin to forget the way he'd brought her coffee in bed, forget the way he could put her at ease with a simple look, forget the way he smelled. Why couldn't he leave her alone for ten more days?

He whirled her around then, bending so they were nose to nose. "April, I'm trying to tell you how I feel about you. Okay, so I'm mucking it up, but, believe it or not, I'm new at this sort of thing."

"Oh? And how do you feel about me?"

"How do I . . . ? Haven't you listened?" With a strangled groan, he pulled her back to the table, then onto his lap. She struggled to stand, but he held her fast. "I've never met anyone like you. You push yourself so far, and inspire everyone around you to do the same. But more than that, you've taken every one of my theories about relationships and dashed them to bits."

Her gaze dropped to the floor. "I-I'm sorry."

He placed two fingers beneath her chin, prodding her to meet his eyes. "I'm not. I needed the reality check. You were right. I thought I knew all about responsibility and what was important in a marriage, but the truth was that at the first challenge, I failed."

"Jeff, you didn't—"

"No," he said, cutting her off. "Let me finish. You tried to tell me that it takes two people to make or break a marriage. Emma and I both failed; I know that. You opened my eyes to that. I need to try again. Not with Emma. With you. I want to spend the rest of my life treating you the way you should have been treated since the day you were born. Like it or not, you're my darling, April. Give me a chance to show you how very special you are. All you have to do is say yes."

With difficulty, she swallowed a lump she was pretty sure was her heart. He couldn't possibly mean what he said. Could he?

"Say it, April." He prompted her. "Will you be my darling?"

Silence reigned for eons. April's expression transformed from one of disbelief to go-ahead-and-kick-me-when-I'm-down, deflating Jeff's confidence. Didn't she realize his sincerity, how much he truly cared about her? By now, she had to know he was no Svengali using false affection as a weapon.

So why did her current indecision dash his hopes against boulders? Plain and simple, because he flat out loved her. April touched him in a way no other woman had—not even Emma. He couldn't quite put his finger on what she offered that lured him to rashness. Sure, she had luscious curves and a smile that sent his heart into a free fall. But there was more to April than sinuous hips and a set of straight white teeth.

Something intangible spoke to him, an undeniable attraction she drew from some deep well inside him. Whatever power she wielded instilled a hunger only she could satisfy.

Had he scared her off? Said too much? Maybe she still thought he was the arrogant yutz she'd first met on the set of *Taking Sides.*

"Maybe we should forget about this," he said, and turned toward the hallway. A run would be good right now. It would give her space and him the opportunity to escape.

"Yes." Her whispered agreement drove a nail straight through his back and into his heart.

Never turning to face her, he offered her a solemn nod and headed for the bedroom for his sneakers.

"No," she called out. "Don't go. What I mean is yes, I want to be your darling."

His hand gripped the doorjamb, and he leaned inside the room again. "You do?"

"Mmm-hmm." His disbelief must have shown on his face, because she nodded like one of those bobble-head dolls. "I'm not afraid of you, Jeff. I could never be afraid of you. Well, now, technically that's not true, because I have to admit I was terrified of you that first day on the set with Jocelyn and Grant. I mean, you looked so put together, so polished, and I was sitting there like one of those kissing fish with my mouth open and nothing coming out . . ."

His darling was now an oil gusher, spewing words so quickly he barely understood her. Then, suddenly, she stopped and stared down at the wood grain of the table. Her nervous fingers picked at a stray crimson thread on her sweatshirt.

"But I *am* scared. I haven't . . . been with . . . anyone since Peter left me. And I've never been with any other man but Peter." She looked up at him then, raw pain rounding her eyes and setting a quirk to her lips. "What if I've forgotten how to love someone?"

Relief eased his taut muscles. "I'll remind you."

"What if I'm no good at it? I mean, that's probably why Peter left me in the first place, right? Because I was a lousy wife? What if I disappoint you too?"

"You haven't disappointed me yet, April."

He sat beside her. When he took her hand in his, his flesh registered how cold she felt. *Wow. She must be scared out of her wits to have her body temperature plummet so much. No problem.* The sparks she sent his way threw his thermostat into overdrive, giving him enough heat for both of them.

Leaning forward, he kissed her slowly, tenderly, with all the adoration stored inside his soul.

When he broke away, the words flew from her lips on a chorus of angels. "Yes, I want to be your darling. If you really think you can put up with me."

He exhaled with all the force of a man made to hold his breath underwater for days. "Put up with you? No, sweetheart. I told you.

I intend to worship you. To discover your dreams one by one and spend my life making them come true."

She sighed and snuggled closer to him, and he kissed the top of her head.

"Do you think you can put up with that?"

"I'm not sure," she purred. "But I definitely look forward to trying." Her head tilted up, and she gazed at him, a smile of sheer joy on her face. "You know what?"

"What?"

"This is the best first date I ever had."

Chapter Thirty

Bright and early Monday morning, David arrived with the union employees responsible for rewiring the cameras. A smiling, fully at ease April offered the production crew coffee, and David's gaze swung from her to Jeff.

"I'll be a son of a . . ." He winked at Jeff and then took the offered cup with a blinding grin. "I knew it would work."

April cocked her head, studying him from every angle. "Knew what would work?"

"Nothing," he replied airily, and sauntered off to oversee the camera setup.

"Jeff?" April asked. "What was that all about?"

Frowning at the empty spot where David had stood a moment before, he sighed. "Promise you won't get mad."

Curiosity overrode April's common sense. "Yeah, sure, whatever. What's going on? What am I missing?"

Jeff took both her hands in his, rubbed his fingertips against her palms. "Remember when David walked me out to the woodpile on Friday?"

"Yes . . . ?" Where was he headed?

"Well, he suggested I use our downtime to warm you up toward the cameras."

A cold chill crept over her. "You mean . . . ?" She couldn't finish the thought, didn't dare follow the trail her imagination blazed.

"No," he said quickly. "I don't mean anything. David's suggestion had nothing at all to do with what happened between us." He gripped her hands tighter, leaned close until they were breaths apart. "Believe me, April. Please?"

193

God, she wanted to! She didn't want to think that all they'd shared in the last twenty-four hours was part of his "love and consideration" game. But could she believe him? Did she dare? She pulled her hands from his grasp and backed away.

His eyes registered hurt, then anger. "You're making a mistake, April," he warned. "Don't do this."

"I'm not doing anything right now." She took several shaky breaths, hoping to regain her equilibrium. "I can't. If I'm wrong, I'm sorry, Jeff. Really. But I need to think. I need to put this in perspective. Unfortunately, I won't get the opportunity right now. We have a show to do. So for now, I'm going to sit on that couch over there and pretend that nothing's happened between us. *Nothing.* When we're alone again, we'll talk. That's all I can promise you."

He nodded, his expression solemn. "All right."

She believed him.

That suddenly, the idea struck her like a wrecking ball, destroying any wall of mistrust David's snide remarks had tried to build. If Jeff had wanted to string her along, he could have made up some ridiculous story. Instead, he'd told her the truth. She believed him.

"David," a member of the production crew called out, shaking her out of her musings. "We're ready over here."

"Great," David replied, then turned to the two of them. "Let's do this, guys! Big smiles. Lots of drama. Give the folks at home something to talk about. Come on."

April strode to the couch and took her seat. When Jeff sat beside her, she picked up his hand and brushed a kiss across his knuckles.

"I believe you," she whispered, and he squeezed her hand tightly in reply.

They sat together, hands linked below the camera's line of view, and waited for the morning's torture to begin.

Normally by this time, April would have to sit on her hands to keep from biting her nails to nubs. Today, though, nervousness didn't hold her in its grip. How could it? Without the cameras all weekend, Grant and Jocelyn would have no fodder to lob at her.

As a matter of fact, the only emotion running through her at the moment was idle curiosity.

Why did *Taking Sides* even bother to showcase them today? A lack of cameras translated to a lack of sensationalism for Monday's audience. So what did David and his production team expect to achieve this morning? What on earth could Grant and Jocelyn find to talk about? Would they rehash some nonsense from the prior week?

Who cared? Nothing could destroy her happy mood today. She was Jeff's darling. Tingles fluttered inside her whenever she considered her new status.

Oh, sure, she'd grown accustomed to the coffee in bed—her favorite decadence. Still, Jeff seemed to have an endless array of ways to spoil her, none of which she'd seen in his book. He found her spa box and gave her not only a pedicure, but a deep-tissue massage to her shoulders and feet as well. She found love notes in her dresser drawers, on her pillow, with her breakfast. Most of all, they *talked*. They shared childhood dreams, laughed over silly disappointments, and planned a future outside the walls of Harmony House.

For the first time in her life, April knew how a pampered princess felt. Yessiree, a girl could get very used to this sort of treatment, but she vowed not to let the indulgences go to her head. This time, she wouldn't dive into love headfirst. Jeff seemed to understand her hesitancy and promised they'd take all the time they needed to really know each other.

"Three, two . . ." David's countdown jolted her back to the present. When he gave them the "on air" sign a second later, the light above the camera glowed, and Jocelyn's voice pierced the silence in April's earpiece.

"As you may recall, technical difficulties kept us from speaking at length with Dr. Jeff and April on Friday morning. Those technical difficulties only increased after we left you a few hours later. We were forced to turn off the cameras at Harmony House for the entire weekend."

The groans from the audience reminded April of a pack of snarling dogs. Did these people really care that much about two total strangers? Why? Was it, as Jeff had told her on their first day together, that the voyeuristic nature of reality television fooled viewers into believing themselves connected in some way?

"Hold on, everyone," Grant shouted above the din. "It's not as bad as you think. Isn't that right, Jocelyn?"

Jocelyn's cat-that-ate-the-canary reply of "That's right, Grant," sent April's stomach into a free fall.

Oh, God. Somehow, she and Jeff had miscalculated. She didn't know how, or what they'd missed, but her belly churned with growing panic.

"We may not have video, ladies and gentlemen," Grant said, "but we have some very interesting audio."

Crash! April's stomach catapulted to earth with enough force to propel her off the couch. Only Jeff's grip on her arm kept her from bolting.

"Sit still," he hissed through a fixed grin. "It's going to be okay."

How could he say such a thing? David had set them up! He might have turned off the cameras, but he'd kept the microphones on. Thus, every single time they'd opened their mouths, believing in full confidentiality, their conversations, their intimate details, their secrets had actually been shared with the entire production team. No doubt David and his cronies had spent most of last night dicing and splicing those secrets for the titillation of a national audience. Mindful of the cameras watching her, she stifled the groan rising in her throat.

Which incidents from their supposedly hidden weekend would take center stage now? A thousand sound bites echoed in her head, each one more devastating than its predecessor.

It was no wonder Jeff didn't seem to mind. Most of his dark secrets were revealed outside in the woods, where no microphones lurked. She'd bared her soul right here on this couch!

Oh, God, oh, God. What should she do?

Jeff's fingers tightened on her hand, but she still couldn't stifle the panic rising in waves, drowning her lungs, making breathing impossible. What would they lead with? And how far into her life would they plunge?

Before she could settle on one particular moment from her weekend's Hall of Shame, Jeff's recorded voice answered her unspoken questions.

"I think you need to lie down."

"No!" The raw need in her voice was unmistakable, and she cringed on hearing such desperation from her own mouth. "Don't leave me. Please."

"I meant *we* need to lie down. If that's what you want."

Ugly whoops and roars resounded from the audience. Aflame with humiliation, April could do nothing but burn while the camera recorded every shade of pink that crept into her face.

"Yes."

Why did they have to make her sound so needy, so pathetic? They didn't even show the emotional breakdown she'd suffered seconds before Jeff offered to take her to bed. As much as she didn't want to advertise her son's disability, she hated the idea that these people would think her some kind of publicity-hungry man-eater instead. Unfortunately, Grant and Jocelyn seemed in no particular hurry to get her out of the spotlight.

"Tell us what happened next, April," Jocelyn twittered.

April scanned the kitchen for the fire extinguisher she knew lay hidden below the sink. If only she could get to that emergency kit and douse the heat in her cheeks.

"N-nothing happened." Jeers and boos greeted her denial. "It's true," she insisted, but she might as well have tried to outroar a hurricane.

Footstomps thundered, catcalls whistled, and April's composure crumbled. Tears poured from her eyes in a flood; her entire body shook with a rage she couldn't control.

"E-nough!"

Jeff's bellow silenced the room with the same effect as a nuclear explosion.

God, how he wanted to take April in his arms and shield her from the smarmy innuendo Grant and Jocelyn delighted in spreading. But he knew that would only inflame them more. The best he could do was defuse the entire situation.

"Why, Dr. Jeff." Jocelyn's acerbic tone cut in. "I don't believe we've ever had quite an outburst from you before. Would you care to explain what has you upset?"

"Quite frankly, Jocelyn," he replied, "*you* do. You and Grant and David Darwin. I'm astounded you show no shame in having misled April and me in such a despicable manner. This kind of fraud was not part of our agreement with *Taking Sides.*"

"Relax, Dr. Jeff." Jocelyn giggled. "We'll get to some of the things you said and did in the last few days as well. Right now, though, I'd like to hear what happened between you two in the bedroom."

"I'll save you the trouble, Jocelyn," he retorted. "April and I, believing ourselves completely alone for the weekend, let down our guards. We discovered a mutual respect and admiration for each other. Those feelings, in turn, led to affection."

The whoops started again, but he glowered the studio audience into silence in short order.

"April Raine is an amazing woman. In all my life, professionally and personally, I've never met a smarter, stronger, and more resourceful individual. I'd like to say I'm sorry for all the trouble I've caused her over the last few years, but I'd be lying if I did."

He flashed a quick smile to reassure her that he hadn't lost his mind. Good thing too. She looked about ready to check his temperature.

"The truth is I'm extremely grateful that my arrogance about a list of family-unfriendly businesses allowed me an opportunity to spend time with April."

"Really?" Grant asked. "Would you care to elaborate on that, Dr. Jeff?"

"When I first agreed to the Harmony House challenge, I assumed that I'd teach April a few lessons about priorities and family." For further assurance, he picked up April's hand in his fist and squeezed gently. "I'm thankful to admit I was wrong. In just over two weeks here, I've learned more about relationships than I learned in all my years at Harvard."

Based on the complete silence that followed his narrative, he assumed he'd left Jocelyn and Grant nonplussed—a bonus, as far as he was concerned. Leaving those two speechless made him feel like a hero.

SuperShrink to the rescue, ready to save a lady's virtue. And thinking of virtue . . .

"April is one hundred percent accurate when she tells you that nothing inappropriate happened between us over the weekend or at any time in the last couple of weeks. I want that known up front so that no one believes I have an ulterior motive for what I'm about to say."

"You . . . mean . . . you're not done yet?" Grant asked.

"No, I'm not." He didn't look at April now. All of his focus remained fixed on the red eye of the camera. "I'm conceding the challenge."

April's hand fell from his clasp. "No, Jeff, don't—"

He faced her, picked up her hand, brushed a kiss across her knuckles. "Yes." After another quick squeeze of reassurance, he directed his attention back to the camera and the world beyond. "You see, I first wrote *Love Is a Contact Sport* to—"

April suddenly threw herself across his lap and fixed her lips on his. The audience roared their approval, but the noise barely registered in his head. April's enthusiastic kiss stole the breath from him. For someone so embarrassed a few minutes earlier, she'd certainly overcome her shyness in record time.

She released him from the lip-lock, and while he inhaled, she pressed her lips to his earlobe. "Don't," she whispered for him alone. "Let Emma rest in peace."

With a quick wink, she returned to her upright position beside him.

"Wow, April!" Grant exclaimed. "That was quite a demonstration. Now, Jeff, you were saying . . . ?"

He took one last glance at April, who clamped her lips into a tight line. "No. That's it. I'm done," he said.

To emphasize his statement, he unclipped his mike and tossed it on the sofa cushion beside him.

Chapter Thirty-one

The limousine ride home was far different from the ride to Harmony House a month earlier. April sat wedged against Jeff and couldn't care less about the highway lines outside the window—or anything else outside the window, for that matter. Jeff had one arm wrapped around her shoulder, and his fingers played with her nape, sending tingles through her blood.

"How do you think your family's going to react to the sudden appearance of a new man in your life?"

She sat up and patted his hand. Imagine: he was actually nervous about meeting Becky and Michael. "Don't worry," she said soothingly. "My kids will love the new man. They're the only ones whose opinions matter. And because I love him, they'll love him too."

"Yeah? Think they'll still love him when they find out he's unemployed?"

She cast him a warm smile. "Actually, I don't think he's going to be unemployed for very long."

"Oh? Are you psychic or something?"

"No, I just happen to know about a parenting services organization that might be in need of a top-notch family therapist."

He cocked a brow at her. "I'm listening. . . ."

"Well, it seems there's this doctor guy who keeps listing Rainey-Day-Wife as the most family-unfriendly business in the tristate area. I thought if we offered family counseling along with our other services, we'd not only lose that particular honor, but actually help troubled families who need more than the gift of time. You interested?"

Folding his arms behind his head, he grinned at her. "We'd have to discuss my salary requirements. I don't come cheap, you know."

"I know." Dollar signs screamed in her head, and she frowned. "Nothing comes cheap these days."

His thumb brushed across her cheek, traced her lower lip. She shivered as his gentle touch sent feathers floating inside her.

"You don't have to do this," he said.

She sighed, snuggled closer, heard the rhythm of his heartbeat and took comfort there. "Yeah, I do. I won't have anyone saying you threw the challenge because you and I secretly planned to split the money all along. Or that I somehow coerced you with my feminine wiles."

"Pffft!" He blew his breath out in disbelief. "Not that I would mind if you tried to coerce me with your feminine wiles." He nuzzled her neck, and delicious pleasure washed over her flesh like a warm, scented bath.

"Never mind." She chastised him, biting back a giggle. "I'll donate the hundred thousand dollars to the Down Syndrome Foundation. They'll put the money to good use."

"What about Michael?"

"If business keeps thriving, I'll be able to save enough for Michael's future, a little at a time. No pressure or anything, but if I employ television's famous Dr. Jeff, I'm betting customers will flock to me in droves. Add to your celebrity that your stupid list is now a thing of the past, I don't see any reason why business shouldn't continue to thrive."

"Hmmm . . ."

He stroked his chin and remained thoughtful until she punched his shoulder.

"Ow!" Rubbing the spot she'd assaulted, he gave her a disgruntled look. "What if I want to sign on with another television show looking for a family counselor? Start my list all over again?"

"No way, buddy. No more television for you. Remember? Television's poison to your soul."

He poked an index finger at her nose. "That's why you kissed me on the air earlier, isn't it? To keep me from talking about Emma? You should have let me have my say."

"Why? So you could confess Emma's transgressions on national television? What would be the point?"

"Sooner or later, the truth will come out. It might have been better coming from me than from some news source more reliable than the *Inquisitor.*"

She shook her head. "With luck, no one will ever learn the truth. Besides, I hate to say this, but Emma's sad story is so old, few people would care even if it did get out. Scandals come and scandals go. Take us, for example. This week, we'll be on the front cover of half a dozen gossip rags. By next week, some spoiled actor or rock star will get caught doing something stupid, and we'll become Jeff and April Who. If the news does get out about Emma, we'll deal with it at that time. If it doesn't, why put her family through so much pain? Let Emma's loved ones find what little solace they can for as long as possible."

"Well, then, there's only one more thing I need to know before I sign on with Rainey-Day-Wife."

She snuggled deeper into his arms. "Mmmm . . . What's that?"

"Whose darling are you, April Raine?"

"Yours, Jeff. Always."